OTHER
PEOPLE'S
BEDS

Anna Punsoda (Concabella, 1985) is a writer and translator from German, with degrees in journalism, philosophy, and Classical Thought and Study from the Universitats Ramon Llull and Barcelona. In her journalism, both written and audio-visual, she has collaborated with *El País*, *Catalunya Ràdio*, *RAC1*, *Nació Digital* and *Ara*. She was involved in the creation of *El Nacional*'s cultural supplement *La Llança* in 2017 and, since 2020, has been the editor of *Dialogal* magazine. Her first novel, *Els llits dels altres* (*Other People's Beds*) won the 2018 Roc Boronat Prize and her essay, *Lust*, appears in the *The Seven Deadly Sins* (also published by Fum d'Estampa Press).

Mara Faye Lethem (New York, 1971) is a writer and translator from Catalan and Spanish. She has lived and worked in both New York and Barcelona, and has translated the likes of Javier Calvo, Patricio Pron, Albert Sánchez Piñol, Toni Sala, Juan Marsé and Irene Solà. Her work has been recognized with two English PEN Awards, and the 2022 inaugural Spain-USA Foundation Translation Award.

This translation has been published in Great Britain
by Fum d'Estampa Press Limited 2022
001

© Anna Punsoda, 2018
Original Catalan Title: *Els llits dels altres*
Original Catalan Edition published by Amsterdam (www.amsterdamllibres.cat)
Translation rights arranged by Asterisc Agents. All rights reserved

English language translation © Mara Faye Lethem, 2022

The moral rights of the author and translator have been asserted
Set in Adobe Garamond Pro

Printed and bound by Great Britain by CMP UK Ltd.
A CIP catalogue record for this book is available from the British Library

ISBN: 978-1-913744-07-6

This work was translated with the help of a grant from the Institut Ramon Llull.

**LLLL institut
ramon llull**
Catalan Language and Culture

🎵 FUM D'ESTAMPA PRESS

OTHER
PEOPLE'S
BEDS

ANNA PUNSODA

Translated by

MARA FAYE LETHEM

OTHER
PEOPLE'S
BEDS

That exit sign was my salvation. It had only been half an hour, half an hour and I was out of there, but the visit had left me trounced and I didn't have the stamina to drive to Barcelona. What was it? Just an old house, an old woman and an old story. And yet they could bring everything crumbling down around me.

I was still on the plain, surrounded by thick winter fog. Slowly, absently, I drove onto the old National highway. A few stoplights later, I recognized the gas station on the right-hand side. The store we stole ice creams from while the black guy who worked there ran to save his dog—a little thing with drippy eyes that we would throw rocks at—hadn't changed either.

I remembered the inn, because it was run by the grandparents of a girl who'd been my classmate at school. She was known for her tongue kissing skills and because her brother had hanged himself with a rope and died. Then she left school and the only things I heard about her were dark tales of doctors and boarding schools.

In the Nineties the inn was a nice place, or at least I thought so because it was big and shiny and had machines for fishing out toys with metal arms. But now it was depressing: the front was streaked with filthy water, the hanging sign bearing the family's name was half-rusted away, the obstacle course made of tractor wheels where we used to play was now filled with junk.

The only parking spot I could find was at the end of a row of trucks and I remained seated in the car as I went through my exercises. Five exercises to ground me, to stitch my body and spirit back together, to help me visualize a string running through me from head to toe, binding me. Because when your head gets away from you and your body's out of your control, who knows what you're capable of. Obviously, it was gymnastics for idiots, but anything was better than that feeling.

Silently going through those motions to regain awareness of this body that carried me through space, I walked amid trucks and tractor wheels, and texted Robert to tell him I was running late. It was a two-hour trip and I needed to calm down before I could drive. Don't do anything in this state: that was basically what I'd learned about myself over the last three years.

A cat lingered over a dead bird beside a moldy set of swings underscored by scummy puddles. Though the bird was already too dried out to get any decent meat from, I felt sorry for it and tried to scare away the cat, which was white with black and blonde patches, and so skinny it was hard to look at. I stepped towards it and into the mud, but the cat just retreated slightly, waiting for the moment it could pick on those bones. I was distraught. You can't save a dead bird, I thought, and we only really grieve our own defeat.

When I decided to go into the restaurant at the inn, there were already some men having lunch. A woman led me to a long, wide table all the way at the back. After tossing a paper placemat and some silverware onto the wooden surface, she looked me up and down. I was embarrassed about my dirty boots, even though the floor was filthy, as was the wall that could be seen between the posters of snowy mountaintops and football teams.

"Claustre?"

It was the hanged boy's sister. With some effort I recognized her. She was tall and skinny like she used to be. She had thin straight hair like she used to. The same gappy teeth. But her face had fallen apart. Drooping cheekbones, drooping lips, and sad eyes that sank at the corners with the weight of a thousand tragedies. Just seeing her made me want to turn tail and leave.

"It's been a long time. Do you come back up here often?"

"More lately, because my mother's old and lives alone in my grandparents' house."

"But wasn't that house filled with people?"

"Used to be. My grandparents died after I finished school. Uncle Magí and my two aunts passed on too, more recently. The only ones still alive are Vicenç and my Uncle Jaume, the one who came to church more often. Maybe you remember him, he's in a home in Montblanc."

She sat down at the table with me and called over a young guy from the bar.

"You still incredibly picky about food?"

She asked me that like she'd ask me the time of day. That made me laugh a good, hearty laugh, but it was drowned out by a group of men who were shouting and arguing at another table, and there was a television on in the background. She was so pale, with those dull eyes, and I wasn't sure whether anything I was saying was actually getting through to her.

"No, I eat anything now."

She ordered for us both. And then, tonelessly, lacking the spirit to put intention into her words, she explained that her grandparents were dead, that her father had died too and that her mother was only sort of alive because she'd lost most of her marbles and often mistook her for a dead spinster aunt from Les Borges.

"Your brother was all people talked about at school for a long time. They said your parents had kicked him out of the house. But they also said they'd put you in a hospital. That you'd stopped speaking…"

Never, not in my last years of high school, nor the year I missed later, much less in the times I'd spent in Barcelona and abroad, had I ever stopped to think about what had happened to that strange, ill-fated family from the inn.

"If he hadn't killed himself, maybe I'd be the one gone," she said, finally. She looked at me and I wondered what would be different about this woman if she were dead. "I'm sorry for all the others. But there are things that can't be hidden, don't you think?"

I don't remember at what point we quit talking about her dark past and started talking about me. I'd stopped at that restaurant to obliterate an old house, an old woman and an old story, to do five grounding exercises and take a series of breaths. But I found myself explaining my life to a very tall woman who was often mistaken for the dead, stuck at an inn with the ghost of a brother who, she told me, had hanged himself after raping her.

I had trouble understanding how she could stay there, amid ratty posters and extremely vivid memories; I hadn't begun to understand or digest anything of what I carried inside me until I was far from Lleida and the house I had grown up in.

Everything can be hidden, but there are stories that are like big eagles pecking at your liver. You shoo them away and cover up the wounds as best you can. You learn to walk bent over, pecked full of holes and making do with one arm, as if that were the only way forward. Until the day you want to live and you need both hands.

ONE

In Lleida, across from the old slaughterhouse, there's a hotdog place that now has a fresh coat of paint and some decent furniture, but for years was just a shithole. My father would go there on weekend evenings when he had to take care of me. He would sit at the end of the bar up against the back wall, but the hotdog place had windows for walls, so you could always see him from the street. Maybe that should have made me ashamed, but the truth is it didn't.

At around seven, when I came out of my afterschool English class, he'd already be holding down his regular barstool. Facing the counter, he'd have the newspaper open in front of him and be stirring a mixed drink. We would sit together and he'd tell me news from around the world, stories about the Counts of Barcelona, and the fact that you had to work a lot to do great things in life. We would order hotdogs that neither of us would finish and he had mixed drinks and I had lemonades. When I was sleepy or tired of listening to him he would tell me: "Go home, little mosquito, I'll be there soon." I don't remember him ever getting back before I went to bed.

That's how it was until once, when I was ten or eleven, I told him that I was big now and he shouldn't call me little mosquito anymore. From then on he always called me big mosquito: "Go home, big mosquito, I'll be there soon." But he would stay on, holding down his barstool for hours more. Home was my mother's house. They were separated but she let him sleep there with us so she could keep an eye on him. He stayed in the study and I slept with her because I was scared—according to what my mother told everyone—but I think she was the one who was scared. Either way, we slept together until I turned thirteen and got my period.

When I met my husband it was a struggle to keep myself from sending him to the sofa, because sharing a bed felt suffocating, a return to the placenta, to my first prison—from which bloodshed was the only release.

In those days, my grandmother—my father's mother—would call me on the phone, crying her eyes out. I hated that vile woman because she always insulted my mother, and maybe my mother wasn't a strong, confident woman, but she was the one who wanted to take care of me. My father would leave for long stretches, move in with my grandmother and then come back, each time yellower and fatter, with those sick cow eyes, and each time more suffocated by that vile woman. My mother always—always—took him back in. "He's your father," she would say. And also: "It's not his fault, the doctors say he's emotionally castrated."

That expression made a terrible impact on me, because at my grandparents' farm we slaughtered pigs and I knew that it was important to cut off their testicles so the ham wouldn't smell like piss. Sometimes my father would look at me pitifully and it must have been because of what he was lacking, but from the outside all you could see was his belly, so round and immense that he had to wear his pants down lower and lower. In the past he'd always been well-dressed, with a good part in his hair and toting a leather briefcase as if off to an important job. He was a man who believed in order and hygiene, but his appearance became increasingly pathetic as the distance grew between what he was and what he'd wanted to be. More than a drunk, a bastard or a mental deficient, what I had most trouble accepting was that my father was a failure. Even today, when my husband—a doctor who comes from money—says that someone is a nobody, it's as if he were accusing my father and me, shaming us.

My grandmother wanted me to ask my father not to drink so much. "You have to ask him," she would whimper, "he'll listen to you. Tell him he has to go to the doctor. That if he doesn't cut back, he'll kill himself." I was repulsed by my grandmother's crying. I didn't like to hear my mother's pitiful crying either, but it didn't repulse me like that.

The vile old woman was a revolting curved skeleton. Always touching food with her hands, she shuffled around her unventilated apartment, loaded down with fifty plastic bags, and wore her hair very long and unkempt. When I stayed at her place and my father went out to the bar she would get into my bed, insult my mother and hug me as she cried. Since I couldn't sleep—it's not easy to sleep with a vile woman crying and hugging you—she would give me sleeping pills, and if I couldn't get up the next day she would fly into a rage and shriek at me.

She always told me that my mother had come between her and her son. That she'd turned his head and that's why he drank and hit her, that he wanted to kill her, he wanted to kill her, and that my mother didn't love me, that she only wanted me so she could keep my father tied to her.

The vile woman called me so many times one Saturday afternoon, that I brought it up with him when he and I were doing homework. The truth is we weren't doing homework. We were sitting together at the dining room table because my mother forced us to, but he was reading and I was doing whatever I felt like.

"Dad."

"Ssh."

"Dad."

"Sssssh."

"Dad, Mom and Grandma say you shouldn't drink so much."

"And what do women know, big mosquito? They just want to bust my balls."

And that was the end of that conversation. Later everything got much worse, but in those years he was still an ordinary, calm drunk, and was kind to me. Except for his mother's scenes and my mother's sadness—always my mother's sadness—I found it all pretty normal. He was a father who drank too much and was emotionally castrated. That was why he slept in the guest room and we spent the evenings at the hotdog place until I went home and he came back later and woke up at lunch time. Then he would underline history books with a pen, crack some jokes about sex and politics, and go back to the bar.

Over the years he got to be a regular; when he didn't come home and we went looking for him everybody knew where he was. The hotdog place was his base camp, but when it closed at one, he wasn't nearly done. He would slip off and we'd put on our shoes and our coats over our pajamas to comb the bars. Opening doors, all I'd see was smoke and some men who looked surprised to see us. Only now do I understand the effect it must have had: a forty-year-old woman in the throes of a nervous attack, her eyes puffy, and holding a girl in pajamas by the hand, searching desperately among the video slot machines.

The only work he did was taking out the trash in the afternoons, on his way to the bar. He didn't drop me off or pick me up at places, he forgot my doctor's visits and parent teacher conferences, and spent all his disability money on women and drink. But none of that really affected me. What made me suffer was my mother as she cried: in the car, while she cooked, when on the toilet, and in bed. I am thirty years old and when I cry it still feels like I'm releasing her sadness from those days.

When I didn't want to go to Cal Pila, the farmhouse where my grandparents lived with my uncles and aunts, she would tell me: "What will you do if something happens to me? Can't you see that we need them? That we can't count on your father, that you and I are alone?" We had each other, but she thought we were alone. Even today I'm still not able to separate my mother from a shattering feeling of total exposure and vulnerability. I've had to construct my entire inner fortress without her, and when I have a problem, I can't tell her about it, because she gets easily overwhelmed and I end up being the one who has to comfort her.

I grew up with my soul bonded to hers, and hers was a half-formed soul, one that gripped my small body in bed while we waited apprehensively for my father to come home. Years later we would still approach our apartment along the opposite sidewalk, crossing the street at the doorway, avoiding the renovated hotdog place, now painted in shades of ochre and with a gleaming bar and waiters who knew nothing of that story. She always seemed to feel relief when she spoke about my father, but it always hurt me and filled me with shame. Why didn't he look for some other woman and some other job and some other life that interested him, at least a little, so he could save himself? Why, if he hated her so much, couldn't he put some space between him and his mother? How could we let him fall so far?

I'm unable to have this conversation. I will never know if he hit them or why he let himself go to such an extreme. He robbed me of the opportunity to grow up and confront him about that, and above all to hear him defend himself.

I've always believed, you pot-bellied failure, you pathetic coward with your mixed drinks and your books, that you should've been able to defend yourself.

TWO

Though everyone who went to the bathroom had to pass by my room, somehow no one managed to see. It was always after lunch, when Vicenç took me there to play. Once we were on the bed, I would take off my skirt, those thick stockings I hated because they were scratchy, and my panties. Then, naked, I straddled his belly and chest, fishing with my tongue for the gum he hid inside his mouth. "You're getting better at it," he would tell me.

At first I found his saliva gross, but as the months passed I got used to it. I also got used to his big, hairy thing. And to that anxiety: "Shhh, get dressed quickly, hide, if your mother finds out she'll be very mad at you." I did everything he said because he bought me packs of gum, not just single pieces and because he had a motorcycle and he would take me out for a ride, and because he told me things about a secret girlfriend. Everyone in that farmhouse was scared of his temper, but I was his favorite and I liked that a lot, so much so that I had him say it over and over whenever anyone was listening.

We played like that until sometime later—enough time that I was no longer wearing thick stockings but rather summer pants—my maternal grandmother sent me to wake him up. I know that it was late because he had come home in the wee hours and his entire room on the lower floor of the house stank of alcohol and tobacco. I called out to him softly and he said "my favorite" and he had me stretch out on the bed. I fished gum from his mouth until a little while later my mother opened the door, turned on the light and asked, "Where's Claustre?" I was hiding under the bed, with one leg missing a sandal, pants, and panties, struck dumb by the cold tile on my butt and my panic at being discovered.

I must have moved or made some noise from under the bed, because she found me and said: "But... what are you doing here, like that?" And a little while later, longer than any while before or since, she told me: "Go upstairs, lunch is on the table." I don't remember her saying anything about the situation, which had to raise flags, and I don't remember her saying anything to him, still in the bed. She closed the door again and left, and I wanted to laugh because she'd caught us, and I found that funny. But I wanted to cry from nervousness and fear of what my mother would say to me later about all that, and of what he would say to me for not putting on my clothes fast enough.

But nothing happened. I was expecting to be yelled at and kicked out, as he'd threatened so many times, but he didn't get mad either. He just had me go upstairs where no one, absolutely no one, said a word to me. In those days it was my father who monopolized all the attention at lunch as he was already drinking too much and we were eager to keep him from making a spectacle of himself. Vicenç also took up a lot of attention, fighting mostly with my grandfather, because at almost thirty Vicenç lived like a teenager, going out every night with people increasingly younger and spending money like there was no tomorrow. The people in the other farmhouses would often wonder how the youngest son of such a strict and moral man could turn out so violent and crazy.

That lunch went on and on; I didn't finish what was on my plate as I'd already lost my appetite by then. My mother complained there was no point in spending all her money on doctors and homeopaths if I didn't eat, and everybody agreed with her: "As if you didn't have enough problems with your husband, now you've got Claustre worrying you too." And when I heard my grandparents, uncles, aunts and relatives in a family with various plus-ones saying those things, I obeyed, because I panicked at the thought of them getting angry with me, and because at seven years old I already knew that in this world you can be anything, anything at all, except a burden.

After lunch, Vicenç disappeared, slamming the door while another aunt of mine, a spinster and the most patient of them all, shouted at him because he had quit a job she'd gotten him. The men went to take a nap, the women continued tidying up the house and I went off to play with some mesmerizing plastic puppets. I can't explain why I found them so captivating, especially since as an only child I had to be both audience and puppet master.

Late in the afternoon my mother came into the room and had me sit on the bed. "Listen carefully to what I'm going to tell you, Claustre," she said, and I looked at her and let out a giggle. "It's not funny. I'm very angry," and then I saw that it was serious and that he was right, that I would be in real trouble when they discovered what we'd been doing. They would kick me out of the house.

"Let that be the last time you get into Vicenç's bed. You understand me?' she said. "You have no business in other people's beds." And looking into my mother's eyes in that moment made me feel more terribly ashamed than ever, dizzy and nauseated.

"Don't be mad at me, Mom," I replied, and when she left the room I went back to my puppets, ashamed but ultimately calm because they hadn't yet kicked me out of anywhere.

Since that summer's day, Vicenç no longer squeezed my cheeks or lifted me a few feet off the ground so I could see my great-grandparents in heaven. He no longer treated me better than everyone else. He didn't bring me packs of gum. He didn't tell me secrets. He didn't even remember the motorcycle ride. Having once been the favorite of the strongest, most volatile man in the house, now I was nothing again, forever playing alone again.

That was why, after some time had passed, one day after lunch, I asked him if we could play more games. He said: "No." That we wouldn't play that day or any other. But he didn't ask me. I asked him. And that question would be my death sentence because I would never stop blaming myself for what had happened in that bed.

I wasn't like the child victims in documentaries with their innocent bodies. I had been a promiscuous girl who accepted his games without complaint and asked for more. That's why it happened to me and not some other girl. And that was why we continued to have lunch and dinner at the farmhouse every Sunday and on holidays.

For years I would distrust myself and my memories, because everyone said that I was a very imaginative girl who lived in her own world, and later, a difficult, lying teenager who didn't eat and was obsessed with bad smells and purification. They also said I'd suffered as a witness to my father's downfall and that sixteen is the worst age for that to happen to you, because you already understand things, but you can't yet really process them.

It wasn't until later that I gradually started to put the pieces together. Then came the confusion and sadness, because as the dresses, beds and situations came into focus and I wondered why my mother hadn't protected me enough, it became harder to visit my family. Who knows if the trouble I've had as an adult with loving and letting others love me stemmed from all that confusion, from the fact the people I trusted most were the ones who did me the most harm?

Maybe they weren't to blame, but, as I've repeated to myself many times, I was innocent. The thing is, I couldn't have known that at the time. Because I couldn't count on my father, and my mother and I were alone. If she found out and got mad at me, if she disowned me or kicked me out of our apartment, anything could've happened to me.

THREE

My mother didn't know how to sew and that made things difficult for me every year when the school festival came along, because we put on a play and had to make the costumes ourselves. What's more, the year I was expected to rise to the challenge—because there's an age where we're expected to rise to the challenge—she wasn't feeling well and we weren't able to make do.

My solution was to catch a terrible cold the week of the festival, but it wasn't bad enough and the afternoon before the performance I found out that they going to make me go, and I still didn't have a costume. Since my part was the nosy fairy Tinkerbell, who stalked Peter Pan and never shut up, I thought of using an old paper lamp we had in the closet. Couldn't I just cut it at one end and get inside?

After jumping on it for a while I finally got it open, but when I wanted to show my mother, she was asleep on the sofa. I shook her and yelled at her but couldn't wake her up. She'd been exhausted for some time—sad and exhausted, as she always said—because having two children in the house is tiring, especially when one of them is your daughter's father.

I was hoping she'd say: "That's pretty shitty but I guess it'll do," like she always did, but there was no way I could get her to react. She slept and slept, out somewhere beyond this life. After a long while of desperate shaking, she finally woke up and looked at me without focusing, letting one hand drop. She paid no attention to my costume, as if she didn't understand the gravity of the situation.

"Put on your shoes, we're going to Cecília's house," she muttered.

Cecília was a neighbor who was very fond of me. We spent many afternoons together and I would sleep over at her place when necessary—and there were plenty of times when it was necessary due to the tense, unstable situations my parents often found themselves in. Cecília and I would watch game shows on television and then I'd sleep in a bed just for me.

I loved going over there because Cecília did things instead of making do. She wouldn't just beat a few eggs to fill my stomach. She'd make me an omelet. She didn't just run a brush through my hair so I'd look half-decent. She would actually do my hair. In that house everything wasn't just an obstacle course. Life was filled with all sorts of things, in fact the same things as in my mother's house, but we did them with joy and tranquility, not running away from something I didn't understand to chase after something else I could never quite comprehend either.

That day, when we arrived and I explained my situation to her, she rushed to rip up some old clothes that'd belonged to her daughter—by then grown up and studying in Barcelona—to make me a costume.

"Stay still now," she said. And she started marking the fabric with straight pins while she spoke with my mother, sad and exhausted there on the sofa.

"You can't go on like this. He'll drag you down with him," she said to my mother. And then they were both silent. "For the love of God, Montse, think about Claustre. You're responsible for an eight-year-old girl," she continued, but my mother didn't answer because she was holding up her forehead with both hands.

Cecília cut some slits in the red skirt she'd made, and underneath sewed long pieces of white fabric. It looked like a cleaning rag, but I didn't complain, as there is nothing worse than a kid complaining when a grown-up has a headache.

"And get a new psychiatrist. It's always good to have a second opinion. Those pills you're taking are too strong. They knock you out."

I was feeling worse and worse as Cecília progressed with the sewing machine, because the first problem with the school plays was always the costume, but the second problem, and probably the bigger one, was the play itself. I was afraid I would bungle my part and screw up other people's too. Afraid I'd fall on stage, stutter my two lines, piss myself in front of an audience. Besides, I didn't ever know whether my mother and father would be amid all those parents watching us, or even if they would be proud of me.

Sometimes they came and sometimes they didn't, but I never knew for sure ahead of time. And going out on stage without knowing if someone was there to see me made me incredibly nervous. So nervous that I wanted to burn down the theater, the entire school, with my classmates and the kind parents who drove me home still inside, and just watch more and more game shows with Cecília before she tucked me into a bed all my own.

That night I couldn't sleep and the next day I really wasn't feeling up to it, but I was so tired that I didn't even care. My eyes closed in class, on the bus, at home; I imagined the theater in flames.

"What's up, little mosquito? How'd the party go?" my father said that evening, unpacking his suitcase in the guest room.

I didn't even have a chance to answer. They kicked me out of the room and started yelling because that week my mother had gotten bad reports and getting bad reports meant yelling all week. It was true that my father had been to the doctor, just as he'd sworn, but he'd gone there drunk, so drunk that he just laughed and slept during the treatment, and the doctor was so fed up with him that he stopped. That was the end of those doctor's visits, and they were going to send him to a special center.

"Watch it or you'll come back to find I've changed the lock," she said to him after a little while. He came out of the room as she was shouting: "Sure, go ahead, go to the bar!"

He left the house before I could explain that it hadn't been a party, it was a play. Yet how could I explain it to him? I would try harder, I really would try harder, I swore. But even though I'd stammered and it was probably better that they weren't there watching me, I'd really been hoping they'd come.

FOUR

I came and went by bus every day to my fairly prestigious private school on the outskirts of the city, but one day my mother came to pick me up. We were going to visit my father at the center where they were 'repairing' him.

The Pines wasn't the clinic I'd been imagining. It was a two-story house near Juneda that had a back garden separating it from the fields. After going up three or four very long, flat stone steps, there was an entryway that stretched out and led to a patient-only area. To the right of the entryway were the doctors' offices, and to the left was a visiting room, which was also very long and had large windows cut into one wall.

They had us fill out some paperwork and sent us to the left. All the families were sitting on a sofa that ran the length of the visiting room and the patients sat in front of them in large chairs. My father took a long time to appear and, when he did, he was unshaven and didn't seem happy to see us.

"How's it going, mosquito?"

"Don't you have anything to tell your father?"

It was all very strange. No coins clinked in his pant pockets and he wasn't leaning forward in his chair, as if about to leave.

"You see, Claustre? They've got me locked up here like a thief."

"Don't say stupid things to the girl."

"It's a joke, mosquito. They just need to give me an oil change."

I'd missed him.

The Pines was a workshop, he explained, and they would keep him here until he was fixed. Spread out in his chair, he was wearing a sky blue sweatsuit that I'd never seen him in before: it was like something a Russian would wear. Then they talked about money. They also talked about my grandmother, about money, about gay Doctor Kong—flaming, my father always said—and then they talked about his liver, and about me, who had been asking after him a lot but now wasn't paying any attention to him. I didn't like sitting across from him like that to talk. I wanted to take him back home with us. We used to talk while drinking at the hotdog place, or while reading the encyclopedia, or imitating Louis Armstrong, talking just to talk, that wasn't something we'd ever done.

An old nurse, or maybe he was a janitor, came over to us and told my mother that Doctor Kong was waiting for her. "Does your daughter want to go out into the garden?" he asked. But my mother said: 'No.' I'd lived through the whole process, she said, and I'd sit with her.

My mother would always look at the doctors as if they were from some other world. "What do you think, doctor?" she would ask solemnly. "How does it look? I trust you completely."

They would then explain details of his illness and she would nod, and say: "But what can I make him for dinner? What can he digest most easily? How many hours should he sleep?" She never shifted from there. Not even the final decline changed her perimeter of anxiety, focused on life's basic functions. And so, while a drunk erratically came and went from our house, making any routines or restful places impossible, she would spend her rather modest salary on the best meat at the market.

"Pere's brain structure is very affected," Doctor Kong told us again. "And that's why his abstinence syndrome is so aggressive. Alcohol has an inhibiting effect and when we remove it his entire nervous system gets out of check." Seeing our faces, he decided to add: "In any case, the hardest part is behind us now."

I couldn't tell you how many times we'd gotten past: "the hardest part." But a moment came when we would rather he kept drinking. Because during the first few days of cold turkey he would sweat a lot, weep loudly, panic over imaginary things and say that his heart was going to explode. And he had crusty scabs on his lips, in the corners of his eyes, and his armpits. Curling up on the floor, he was a most pitiful sight.

I've seen dying children, schizophrenics making scenes, and old people shitting themselves, but I've never seen anything as sad as a grown man of fifty crying and shaking like a dog. "Stand up and protect me," I tell him now when I remember him kneeling there in the corner. But at the time all I felt was grief, a grief that fell onto me and buried me slowly, bit by bit.

I don't know if there are less aggressive treatments now, but in the Nineties rehab for alcoholics consisted of cleaning out their bodies. They detoxed them, as they called it, but they didn't repair their nervous systems, and so they were unable to concentrate and relate to other people. The fastest route back to a normal life for my father was returning to the bar. And once he was there he drowned himself in the process, stewed in his well of shit.

"What can I make him for dinner? What can he digest most easily? How many hours should he sleep?" We didn't dare even look at the other subject, the problem behind the problem.

When, the week after, my mother told me we were going back to The Pines, I said: 'No.' Not because it was hellish having to converse in that room. Not because it was tedious to listen to the doctors, who lied routinely, the way we all do when we aren't getting to the crux of things. But because when we left Dr. Kong's office I saw my father heading down the entryway hall. Before he went through the door that led to the patients' rooms, disguised in his blue sweatsuit, he mimed playing the trumpet, to make me laugh. What a wonderful world, he would sometimes sing, moving his chubby fingers.

I've never forgotten the sadness of that door. It was the first time I wasn't there for him. And by the time I wanted to shout out for him not to worry, that I had been listening closely, very closely and for the time being we hadn't changed the lock, he was already gone.

FIVE

I spent recess up against the radiator in the silent chapel that was inside the church on the right-hand side. I sat there for many months, until a catechist found me and blabbed about it to my teacher, who interrogated me for almost an hour. Mr. Puiggròs was a short, stocky man with folds on his arms that were filled with filth and lint, and a few strands of hair combed over his bald pate. He'd been studying for the priesthood but in the end he'd found a giant, maternal parishioner who married him, moved by the intimacy they'd discovered cleaning the church. Puiggròs spoke like the priest he had never been, but with the smugness of someone who believes he knows something about life because, unlike many of his colleagues, he had actually fornicated.

To get out of his office I told him that I would go to the church and pray to calm my mother's nerves, but the truth is I didn't want to be around anyone else. I didn't know what to say or when to say it, I spoke too much or not enough, or when it wasn't my turn. I hated recess and I hated lunch even more, because eating has always been a problem for me. It wasn't that I didn't like having tastes in my mouth. What I don't like is swallowing. Or eating with people. And what I hate most is when other people serve my food. At fifteen I made a pact with my mother: I would eat, but only what I myself put on my plate.

When they discovered my religious hideout at school, I started hiding in the bathrooms. The school was very large, so I could move between them. The preschool bathrooms, the primary school bathrooms, boys and girls, the teachers' bathrooms, the visitors' bathrooms, the chaplains' bathrooms. I got used to the bad smells and those dark puddles made by stepping in piss with dirty shoes. It was all going well until a classmate ratted me out and the teacher came to take me straight to the lunchroom. What was I doing, so many hours in the bathroom? I was just in there. I sat on the ground, near the toilet, and looked at the wall. It was enough for me to just not be with the other kids, who might humiliate me at any moment.

Whatever we were playing, when the two popular girls chose their teams, I was always the last one picked and got stuck into whichever group had fewer people. To even them out, they would say. Dead weight, they meant. I stopped playing because I was afraid of being the last one picked and everyone seeing. I wasn't embarrassed that nobody wanted me. I was embarrassed that everyone saw. That they would tell other people. And that those people would tell other people. That in the end I wouldn't be able to leave the house without everyone knowing that I was dimwitted and alone and an outcast.

In third grade a new nurse came to the school. Her name was Luci and even her name seemed very modern and different. Besides, she wore her hair short and dyed orange, a lot of eye makeup both above and below her eyes and had drawn-on eyebrows. I didn't like the previous nurse at all. She was fat and pious, her skin was milky and she always said: "If this girl won't eat more, I can't work miracles." Luci didn't tell me anything. She let me lie down on the stretcher and put hot-water bottles on my belly. They help with everything, she would say. Even when it's nothing.

Thanks to Luci I would spend recess on the stretcher and if anyone came in I pretended to be sleeping. She would tell me things about life, or about her daughter Nàdia, who went to the same school but was four years older than me and was daring and stacked. Sometimes she would come into the infirmary to see her mother. They spoke to each other in Spanish. Her mother would look at her and when they argued—they argued a lot—she would act offended, but you could see that she was happy with her. "What a spirited girl I have!" she would say. And I understood that being firm and saying things loud and clear was what she meant by that. I was so envious of them. I've never seen vocal cords, but I imagine them being different depending on how each person speaks. Luci and Nàdia's were taut while my mother's were droopy and weepy.

"Maybe you'll be a nurse when you grow up," she told me one day. "Since you like to watch me take care of kids who don't feel well."

According to that logic I would also be a nun, and a plumber. I wasn't looking for a career. If someone asked me what I wanted to be when I grew up, I always replied that I wanted to give out ID cards that allowed you to live in Spain, like my mother did when she was feeling well. But they couldn't be cards for very poor immigrants, because to deal with them you have to have the patience of a saint and be really good with people, and I, they said, didn't have either of those virtues.

My mother was very sensitive, too sensitive, a very good person, too good a person, and that was why they had her dealing with North Africans and Russians, because they would cry and tell her all their troubles. She would cry too and say she understood perfectly, that she knew they needed the cards to open businesses, but that the rules were the rules and she couldn't change them. She made a living listening to strangers' problems and explaining to them very slowly, in Spanish with well-enunciated vowels, in that shrill voice of hers, all the absurd procedures and how she too had her 'cross to bear.'

After the Christmas holidays I was anxious and had to skip lunches again. I went straight to the infirmary, but since Luci wasn't there yet I sat on the floor to wait for her, leaning against the door, and looked at the wall.

"Was the vegetable soup good?" she asked me on the second day.

"Yes."

"You're not much of an eater, huh?"

I was shocked. She'd always been so kind, always made me feel so calm, and now she was asking me the same questions that everybody always asked me.

"How come?"

I shrugged.

"Do you find it gross?"

I shrugged again.

"Didn't you have a good Christmas?"

"Yes."

"Is there something going on at home?"

I didn't really understand that question. But since it was Luci asking, I told her the truth, that I had a very big pit in my throat and that was why I couldn't swallow. I opened my mouth so she could have a look and she felt my throat and pointed inside with a flashlight. Apparently there was nothing there but, who knows, she said, maybe when I was a little older they could take out my tonsils, since I was always getting tonsilitis, although for the time being I needed them to protect me from infections. Taking out my tonsils seemed like an obvious, definitive solution, one I hadn't even realized I was looking for.

That afternoon, on my way back from the infirmary, Mr. Puiggròs called me into his office. He said that Jesus was born every Christmas for everyone, including me, and that I had to thank Jesus for my health and my life. He said that my mother worked very hard to bring me up all on her own, and that I should be happy to make her happy, and should thank her for my health and my life. He said that, inspired by God's compassion, the school made an effort to pay for my studies, and that I should be grateful. Jesus, my mother, and compassionate God loved me very much. So much so that I was obliged to show them all love in return. And how do I do that? asked Mr. Puiggròs, before answering himself. Well, by getting very good grades, as I was already doing. Giving and receiving joy. And enjoying the good things in life. Such as my classmates. My free time. The rice with a fried egg on top that the school cook had made for lunch today. And, he added in a very soft voice, as if praying, that if my throat hurt so often, I should see a specialist, but the school infirmary was for occasional minor health issues.

It was as if I were dying. I bit my hands and lips, but my throat hurt terribly. It swelled up like when you blow into a fire. I would not forgive that betrayal. No matter how much pain I was in, I would never go back to the infirmary. Mr. Puiggròs went on for a long time about what a precious gift life is and I couldn't stop thinking: how could she have told him everything?

It was some time before I could concentrate and pretend that Luci was dead to me. I imagined that her brains had spilled out after falling backwards down the school's stone steps, leaving the landing covered in blood and bits of meat. It worked, as it always did when I wanted to make someone unimportant and unable to hurt me.

For the time being, though, I had nowhere to spend recess. And while I thought long and hard about new hiding places, like the shed where the school gardener stored his tools, I realized that I could buy some time by slowly gathering up my books and walking at a snail's pace. That I could drag my feet like a zombie to the lunchroom where, chewing as methodically and slowly as I could, I would swallow everything they put in front of me.

SIX

The granddaughter of the woman who took care of me when I was a little girl was three years younger than me and was hopelessly good-natured, born that way. I can't imagine anything that could corrupt such a heart. Moreover, her grandmother saw only good in me and treated me like a queen so that no one could say that I got short shrift compared to her granddaughter, who in turn was truly devoted to me.

It is with her that I have my first good memories. For many years she was an important part of my world, because my parents didn't pay much attention to me, and we spent many evenings and nights together. It wasn't that I was super bossy, but Letícia was so obedient that I was left with no other choice.

Over the years I started to make her tie my shoes, and she would also tidy up the room for me. She never said no, and always served me with great excitement and kindness until one day, when I was eleven and she was eight, we were playing in the dark, sad living room where her Galician grandpa was watching a football match. That evening I pretended to get a call on the cordless telephone, the kind with a button that made a loud noise so you could find it if it got lost.

"You have to take off your pants."

"Why?"

"Because David told us to."

David was a man I'd invented who had been calling us on the phone for a few weeks and giving us orders. Ever since the day David told her to throw oranges off the balcony and her grandmother screamed furiously at us, Letícia was terrified of him. But even so she took off her pants.

"Now you have to take off your panties."

"But why?"

"Because he says so. If you don't, he's going to show up here and kick us out of the house."

She looked at me in horror with those little eyes of hers, so pure and devoted, and hesitated. I was the older one, and her expression implored me to stop blackmailing her, stop with that terrifying voice that forced us to do stuff she didn't want to do, raised as she'd been by strict, loving grandparents. Finally, crying, she took off her panties. I lay down on the sofa.

"And now you have to lie on top of me."

She took a step back. "No," she answered. And then even as I sat up in surprise and was about to scold her: "I don't want to," she said without hesitation, and she ran out of the living room sobbing loudly and with her butt exposed. At first I was shocked. Then I got really mad. Why didn't she want to? How was that even possible? Who did that pipsqueak think she was, anyway?

David didn't call again, because he'd died when I got yelled at over that cruel and perverted game, and I started to feel isolated from everything, including from Letícia. It wasn't that she'd begun to distrust me, it was that I'd begun to distrust myself. I had been left alone with an old agitation that made me anxious, and under unremitting suspicion from my babysitter. She asked me strange questions and treated me with more distance, as if she could no longer see the good in me because I wasn't her granddaughter and I didn't have as virtuous a heart.

I didn't make her tie my shoes or tidy up the room for me anymore. And a year later I didn't give her up for dead because I loved her a lot, but I did shove her into a corner, in part because I was already big enough to stay home alone without a sitter, and in part because her devotion upset me. Discovering that I could hurt someone and that my only limits were the ones I placed on myself opened up an abyss of insecurities within me, leaving me confused and suspicious of myself.

I never stopped seeing Letícia, but it wasn't until twenty years later that I visited her to talk about all that and ask for her forgiveness. I didn't know if she would even remember it, if in her mind it would be merely a vague memory of some child's play or if it had ruined her life. How could I have invented a voice that made us do all those things?

How could I have had such an imagination? She wanted to know. I don't know. Just as I have no idea why she knew how to escape and I didn't. Or what I would have turned into if that little pipsqueak hadn't gone running out of that room.

SEVEN

A woman was crying because her daughter had hurled herself off some precipice somewhere and was now lying half-dead in the same room as my father, who had drunk himself into a massive hepatic coma. "Lord, lift him up by Your side," said my mother and, examining his yellow face and scabby lips, added: "You don't think he looks bad today, do you, Claustre? You don't think he looks bad, terrible, worse than ever, on his last legs?" And she continued, shaking her head. "You realize you could be left in a wheelchair. Or worse, he could end up a vegetable. A vegetable. We would eventually divorce, but you, you'd be left holding the bag. What would you do with a mummified vegetable for a father? With a paralytic! With a cripple!" Then she looked at the mother of the half-dead girl, covered me in kisses and said: "Now that's a real tragedy, what happened to that woman."

A woman in her forties, a giant with short hair that had been dyed yellow, was sitting in the waiting room of the Arnau de Vilanova Hospital. She came to find me to tell me that she was a friend of Pere Gual's and to ask how he was doing. I explained to her: when your liver doesn't work right your body fills with garbage and my father's body was full of garbage and just then she stopped me because she said that she already knew all that.

The woman told me about people who were dying but that at the last minute came back to life and never drank again. She had an alcoholic friend who one day jumped out of a moving car but didn't succeed in killing herself. Her friend went into a coma and came out fifteen days later and when she got back home she started eating like crazy. Soon she was obese and lost her job but at least she'd quit drinking.

Then she congratulated me for the grade I'd gotten on my university entrance exam and I didn't know what to say because I'd never seen that lady before in my life. Then she told me that she was an entertainer.

My mother came into the waiting room, shot the entertainer a look, and told me that we had to go and get clothes for my father, that he was dying. The entertainer offered to come with us, to do paperwork, make calls, run errands, but my mother only said: "Claustre, tell this woman that such delicate moments are for family only."

So we waited for Teresa, my mother's sister, who at the door to the hospital held me tight and said: "Poor thing," before saying to my mother: "Girl, this will be such a weight off you." Then the three of us went to my grandmother's filthy, disgusting, packed apartment—it was like few I've seen. My father had moved back there to resume writing a thesis that fifteen years ago he'd been really close to finishing, that just needed: "a little whipping into shape." As they stood in the entryway, waving their hands and complaining about the stench, I was able to throw out a newspaper covered in fingernails that he'd left on the telephone table and pick up a cute headband with fuzzy cat ears from the desk.

The two women then went straight into the bedroom and, rummaging through everything to find clothes for a dead man, they came across a white shirt with two thin strips of red sequins that went all the way up the sleeves to the collar. The shirt had a long train and, stitched in gold on the back, read: 'Sex Bomb'. "What is that?" asked my mother. And just then my aunt pulled some black straps out of a drawer, all tangled up in a bunch. "What the hell is that? What is all this?!" shouted my mother. "Ask your crazy-ass husband," said my aunt, who hated my father because on his honeymoon he yelled: "Teresa walks with a limp" down the halls of the Colosseum. And because when my mother told that story every time we had guests, we all laughed heartily, despite her always saying that it had really hurt her. I still think about it now: "Your grandmother is a bitch", "The king is dumber than a bagful of hammers", "Jordi Pujol is a sellout"— of all the war cries he would shout into the valleys of the Pyrenees, that was the only one that made my mother angry.

That evening they were both very anxious because they were saying they wouldn't even be able to give all that stuff away to charity.

What could the poor do with that 'Sex Bomb'? And while they argued over whether we could use the straps to tie up my grandfather in the bathtub—he was a giant and always slipped when we washed him—I put the fuzzy headband in my bag.

When we went back to the hospital, the entertainer was still there. Stock still, she was staring at an ugly painting on the wall. Since only two people at a time were allowed into the ICU, and my aunt wanted to go in there with my mother, I stayed with her. She wasn't pretty, in fact she wasn't attractive at all, but she smiled and she had something that made you want to draw close to her. I asked her how she knew my father, and she told me about some jazz club.

"It's a music club, don't get the wrong idea," she said. "But sometimes I go there with two or three of my entertainer friends. The last time I saw him we argued because he was sitting on a sofa with Marisol... He knew that it would hurt me, him spending the night with Marisol. He did it to hurt me..." Her nose was dripping from the crying so I started rummaging around in my bag for a handkerchief, and when she saw the fuzzy headband I thought she would die of grief. "He always does the most hurtful things. The worst things..." she said miserably.

"There are good things about him too," I said, to get that Marisol out of my mind.

"When he would talk about politics, it was hilarious. Or about the Greek whores. About that moron on the boat who goes to the Greek whorehouses. His wife is the biggest whore of them all: she just waits for him to make him come back. The biggest whore of them all, he would say. She doesn't miss him, no. She just wants him to come back."

We laughed for a little while, talking about how crazy he was and the stories he would tell, all sweaty and red as a lobster—I now realize he was drunk as a skunk—until my mother and my aunt came out of the ICU. They were radiant.

Two days later we buried him at the church where I'd done my confirmation three months earlier. He'd left halfway through the

Mass: "sick of parasites, suckers, and sanctimonious cross-kissers" and anxious to get to the bar. The funeral was informal. A retired friend of his plugged a guitar into the speaker and sang an alternative version of the Our Father.

After *Gloria in excelsis Deo*, his friend went back to the altar and turned on an old cassette player. The tape kept getting stuck and so a jazz club friend went up to help him. They were there for five minutes huddled over it, complaining, showing their hairy backs and butt cracks. *When the Saints Go Marching In* finally started, and I couldn't keep from laughing, imagining him dancing with his big belly and his ridiculous little legs. Who would I dance with now the way he and I used to, flapping our arms in a funky chicken, while Mom yelled at us because we never lifted a finger and the house was a pigsty?

And while I thought about our trip to the outskirts of New Orleans, where Louis Armstrong was born, a trip he'd promised me twenty times but that never happened, the priest asked if anyone in the family wanted to say a few words. We'd agreed that after the Mass I would thank everyone for coming and recite the poem *Cant espiritual*. But the best jazz dancer deserved a different farewell. What did he deserve? Maybe for me to look out at everyone and laugh so hard I cried, red in the face, staggering, and explain to them, as he used to, why anal sex is cleaner than any other kind. "You can't understand it now, big mosquito, but there's no reason to be afraid of the digestive tract, not of people who eat well. On the other hand, the pussy is a very dark lair! The pussy is a black hole, the only one we know. You go in there one night and you never know where you'll come out, years later." And he'd laugh and laugh, like a lunatic.

Or maybe he didn't deserve more buffoonery. Maybe he deserved the truth and, with my grandmother looking at me from the front row, all emotional, I wanted to shout: "If you needed another man, why didn't you go look for one? And not in his bed." But I didn't really know if that vile old woman had gotten into my father's bed the way she had with me, if she'd also hugged him and cried and given him sleeping pills when he was nervous at night.

So I recited the poem we'd agreed upon and halfway through I heard her leaving. Dragging her feet, carrying a plastic bag, scattering her disgusting sobs everywhere, and that was the last time I ever saw her because when they called me years later from a nursing home to tell me she was dying, I didn't show up. I suppose I hated her as much as I can hate anyone because by castrating him with her sick jealousy she had buried a talented person with a capacity for joy. And because everything is hard, and painful, and I can understand someone not wanting to live, someone wanting to destroy their liver in a bar. What I cannot understand is how a woman, no matter how much it sucks to be a widow, could spend fifty years suffocating her only son.

When the vile woman left, the priest said we should go in peace and if we wanted to say goodbye to Pere, laying yellow inside a too-small suit jacket, he would be at the church for another half an hour. The scene lacked any charm since we'd forgotten to buy wreaths, and we made do by surrounding the table covered in cards with some flowers on wheels that they brought in if you paid an extra supplement (we didn't pay, but no one had the heart to cart them away). Then a fat friend of his went up to his coffin and placed a guitar pick inside. An elegant lady left a flower. The owner of the jazz club, some scores.

People came by, left a little something on the table, hugged me, and left. Only the entertainer waited until the end. Wiping away her tears, she put in a white tie that matched the Sex Bomb shirt.

I told her that that would please him, since he always said that the world was full of pansies and there were no real men left. But the woman said: "No," and that "he hadn't been able to for a while." My father was impotent and he chose her—his entertainer—because she was the most discreet and the best at pretending.

Would I keep the secret? Of course, I promised her. And I left her there saying her goodbyes to the coffin in that church where only he remained, marching with the saints, sloshed and out of step. Dancing behind them all with his big belly.

EIGHT

In my thirty years I've bathed in more than a hundred bathtubs. It's a hobby I've had since forever, from my earliest adolescence, because I constantly stink and need to wash more than other people do. Also because in our apartment in Lleida we only had a small shower covered with a plastic screen that got all filthy and gross, so when I stayed over at Cecília's house they couldn't get me out of the water.

Being able to stretch out in there alone, naked, in silence, without my drunk father spying on me and laughing, or my mother shouting because he was spying on me, was a turning point. People were cruel, existence jagged and dirty, but there were bathtubs, round bathtubs, long ones, ones with bubbles and massage features, bathtubs that allowed you to think about the great battles of history and clearly see the path you must choose in this life.

At sixteen I started babysitting little kids from school. At the houses of couples who paid me to watch their children while they went out and had fun, I would put the kids to sleep and then go fill up the tub. I stretched out for an hour until I was immaculate, entirely clean, and had mapped out the next few days in my mind: the university entrance exam, all the classmates I hated, a lie I'd told my teacher that'd forced me to forge some paperwork, the workshop where they'd sequestered my father, the doctor they wanted to take me to. Everything mixed together in my head, but in a bathtub things became clearer and I could organize them in order of importance.

I found my favorite tub at my English teacher's house, known in the city because he came from a rich family and married a young widow who loved her first husband more than him. Everyone said that she still loved the dead man and that if she hadn't been a Catholic who wanted to embrace Christ's suffering, and if Ricard hadn't been rich or hadn't had his face marked by some strange illness, he never would have been able to fill the shoes of her first husband.

But he looked like a colander, and so the fact that they had a pair of such good-looking kids was a miracle. And a fluffy dog, an expensive car, a large house. They also had, and this is where I am heading with all this, an immense bathroom and a freestanding bathtub with two backrests. I soon figured out how it worked and, stretched out there, nice and long, covered with water and bubbles, and with my skin almost melting, I imagined that I was losing all the fat off my body and that I lived free, abroad.

Ricard had always valued me because I have a talent for languages and because one day I asked him about the marks on his face. Explaining how they came about and how everyone had tortured him as a teenager brought us closer. So much so that in June, when I finished high school, he asked me to take care of his kids, and that was how he became the first of my friends. For years "friends" meant men I was in love with, because I didn't know how to differentiate feelings. This led me to secretly enter the most shameful beds, creating a permanent separation between my intimate and my outer life.

The first night of our friendship I had put his children to bed and gone to fill up the bathtub. When I was stretched out inside it, I heard the front door and some footsteps that came running all the way upstairs. Since the penitent widow was out of town visiting her parents, it could only be him.

"Excuse me," I said, covering myself as best I could with a towel.

"Go ahead, no problem."

"It's just that Carlota puked on me and I wanted to shower."

"Of course," he said, and came closer to me.

He pulled off the towel and we began a ritual that we would repeat over two long months. We always followed the same procedure: once we were naked he would kneel and lick me down there for a little while until my legs got weak, which was when he would gather me up in his arms, take me to the bathtub and there we had sex—once, almost twice.

At the time I didn't explain it like this, because my body was a stranger to me, but I can't orgasm. I've tried on my own, with an artist, with a woman who was a retired geography teacher, with men

I loved and with others I didn't care much about at all. I've tried both without thinking about it too much, trusting it would just happen, and the other way round: devoting an entire hour to the effort. And nothing. My body is poorly constructed. There is a moment when I need to stop, no matter what, because I go from pleasure to stabbing pain. It's as if a dog is biting me down there, or is about to.

I explained that to Ricard as best as I could, but he didn't want to believe it. He took it as a challenge and went around looking here and there, consulting specialists, asking me every second if we were getting close. We almost stopped seeing each other over the whole thing. I just wanted to stretch out in the bathtub, to not stink so much and feel the warm water. And if he was there, I was fine with him touching me, but I didn't want him to turn my body into some sort of experiment. Sex wasn't invented to cause problems. "If it can't solve anything for me, at the very least I don't want it to cause me any problems," I explained to him. And then he would get mad because he said I had such low expectations from life and people, and that my attitude was offensive to those who loved me.

One day when we were together, his young daughter came into the bathroom. She had woken up in the middle of the night and when she saw us in the bathtub she wanted to play with us. Her father rushed to cover himself, as if he feared he'd be fined. "A child shouldn't even imagine their parents' genitals," he said afterwards, and I felt a happiness that slowly expanded within me. The colander was old, perverse deep down like his entire species, but he was raised better than my father and all my uncles.

Thanks to him I got a job at an English language academy, and though I no longer needed to babysit, I continued to bathe at his house. Maybe that was why, and because I felt bad accepting his money, that one day he called me up to tell me that it was over. That he was getting divorced and would look for a large apartment with a bathtub, not because I stank, that I didn't at all, but because he loved me and was tired of long-suffering women. He wanted me to be able to just devote myself to university, abroad if necessary. And most of all he told me not to worry, that he'd heard about an American woman named Dodson who would put an end to my stabbing pains.

I was shocked. It wasn't that it seemed bad to me, not on the face of it. But I needed to digest the information. To think it over, long and hard. And since the holidays were approaching and we didn't have work at the English school I decided to shut my phone off for a few days.

"When you were at the library a man came asking for you," said my mother, a few days later. "I know him but I can't remember where from. Tall, potbellied, with a scarred face. Who is he?"

My brain started to swell. I had soaked it so much over the previous two months, and it was now starting to swell up again. I felt my skull getting smaller and smaller, its contents inflating. We didn't have a bathtub at home, I no longer babysat, and I wasn't close enough to my co-workers to ask to use their tubs. I didn't know where to stretch out. I didn't know where to take a bath. I didn't know what to do.

I wanted to rest somewhere. Or rest on him. But I couldn't rest on him because I hated him, because the little I had, he had given me and he would soon make me pay for it. My job at the academy, my laptop, my life far from home, imagining a family—where had I gotten those things, if not from him? Everything disgusted me and I couldn't find anywhere to bathe.

I locked myself in my room to try to tidy up my mind. What was happening that was so terrible? That couldn't be resolved? What had changed, in twenty-four hours, that had me so flustered? It's okay, I told myself. And that was true. All I had to do was ask Ricard if we could take it slower. I had to keep working, find a female friend I could talk to, register at the university. There were steps to follow. And I could follow them if I did so in the correct order and didn't get muddled up.

I was in a good position, actually. My relationship with Ricard would allow me to leave home without looking like I was abandoning my mother. Men have always played that role for me. I could go back occasionally, or very occasionally, and comfort my mother who, ever since my father had died, employed more emotional extorsion than ever. I flailed my arms in broad strokes to make my way and push her aside, but she would come back, talk about my father and how alone we were. She mostly talked about some blocked feelings I supposedly had, feelings she wanted me to express. How could I explain it to her? The only blockage I had was fat and my only serious problems were my constant stench and those stabbing pains down there.

She knocked on my bedroom door to call me for dinner. "Who was that man who came by?" she asked, passing me some soup. Nobody, I said. Some guy I met, and she started to talk about the head of her department, a very rich woman whom I hated and she loved: "despite the fact that she never so much as lifted a finger." Because some months back, when my father was still alive and sick, she'd helped my mother find doctors who were, as my mother said: "beyond our means."

"But can't you tell me who he was? Why don't you ever tell me anything?" she asked me again. But I was silent and she went on, about her job, her boss, her boss' daughter, who was my age and studied in Barcelona. A young woman so capable and sharp that she would soon move to London, who had a great future ahead of her but who hadn't made much progress in Lleida.

"I couldn't live without you," she said suddenly. And it was as if someone destroyed me from inside, leaving my head and legs numb and dead.

NINE

The effect intelligence has on us when we aren't used to it might explain what meeting him meant to me. When I talked to Lluís my brain grew, and everything I'd learned up until then, which was a lot—much more than he knew, I see now—gradually made sense and began to fit into some sort of system.

When he talked, he gleamed with brilliance. He was clever. Very cultured. He was a demanding conversationalist. Every once in a while, he would make some sarcastic remark about my appearance not being very elegant, or about the goat farm where I grew up, and even though it hurt me, I never said anything to him about it. Lluís was the first person I ever wanted to prove something to and, as much as I hate this idea, I think we always aspire to be what that first person who dazzles us wants us to be.

That he still lived with his parents at thirty years old didn't surprise me at all. Or that after finishing an architecture degree he'd decided he wanted to be an interpreter. That even though he didn't work I'd never seen him wear the same clothes twice didn't surprise me either. His confidence explained a lot of strange things.

By the time I spent the first night at his apartment, it was already overdue. We'd been a couple for four months and hadn't slept together, in part because we had nowhere to go and in part because I was very happy not to be having sex. There were the stabbing pains. And besides, there was all that with the gum and the cold tile on my butt, and merely linking that to my adult life made my brain stop. A short circuit, a head paralysis, that stuttering. I could think about everything except that, and had to keep it far from me by any means necessary, especially then, when I had managed to get to university and to Barcelona.

With Lluís I had an opportunity to improve, but I was so scared of making a fool of myself that I avoided being naked anywhere near him. I put it off until one day when we went to his parents' apartment,

which was dark and filled with paintings of lemons and people practicing extinct trades. It had a long hallway and his room was at one
end, isolated from the rest of the house. The room was large but the
bed was short and narrow, and when we lay down on it I constantly
felt as if I was falling. I kept juddering as I struggled to stay on the
mattress, then laughed to cover it up.

"Wow, all good?" he said. And I answered: "really good," while I
was mostly just trying not to fall off the bed. I couldn't find any way
to focus on the important task at hand, and I just went along with it
until I don't know how but he put his hand into my panties. Suddenly
he froze. At first I thought he didn't dare, because I wasn't that into
it to let him go so far, but he pulled out his hand, sat up and said to
me, very seriously: "Go wash yourself, you're too wet, and we can't
do it like this."

Dying of embarrassment, I didn't know what to say and so I went
down the incredibly long hallway to the bathroom, sat on the bidet
and washed myself. I went back to his bed and said I was ready. Then
it all went pretty quickly.

We never spoke about that defect of mine. But I gradually lost
the devotion I'd had for him. And when the summer ended and we
started our second year of university, my anxiety returned. No matter
where I was I felt detached and distanced from myself. I couldn't focus,
I couldn't calm myself down, I couldn't even control the perimeter
around me. There wasn't a moment of the day or night—not even at
home, lying in bed—when I could calm down and gather myself. I was
disintegrating amid angst and dangers, and in the end I let myself go.

"I don't have the patience for all these lies," he said. "Go talk
to a psychiatrist, Claustre. I can't take it anymore. You not eating is
serious. But you manipulating me so that I don't eat is the last straw.
Can't you see that something's wrong with you?"

I talked to him about my disintegration and the extorsion and
threats but he didn't want to listen. He'd already decided he didn't
want to understand me. He got up from the table where we were
sitting and he stopped answering my calls. From that day on he never

spoke to me in the department hallways again. He avoided any possible meeting and the circles of acquaintances where I might be.

I didn't love him, and years later I don't think we could ever have loved each other, but him getting up from the table and denying me any chance to explain myself really hurt. The anxiety of that academic year—an inner anxiety with no material reason behind it because they'd given me a scholarship—was exacerbated by the feeling that maybe I'd behaved badly and that a guy I didn't speak to anymore and would never speak to again knew too much about me.

A few weeks later I understood it more clearly. I was sitting with Oriol, a student in our department, when he said: "I haven't mentioned it until now because I didn't know if I should get involved, but Lluís told me about your problem." Lluís was acerbic, classist, and had a limited knowledge of people and how they could be undone by having their shameful worlds exposed, yet I was still incredulous that he could have told anyone.

My fears were coming true, and I wanted to make some excuse, explain that it wasn't really my fault but some involuntary manifestation of my body, and the nerves I sometimes had, but then Oriol coughed and said: "You should get your anorexia treated." Suddenly that fear deflated.

That I lied and didn't eat. That I manipulated him so he wouldn't eat. What did I care if the other students knew that? I felt like laughing. I've won, I thought. But what did I win? And who did I beat? I don't know, I'd just won. I felt utterly victorious each time I'd been afraid someone would hurt me, but then it turned out that they couldn't really touch me where it mattered, because they couldn't see inside me.

It wasn't until I ran into Lluís at the university sometime later that my fear returned. When he looked at me, I told myself that I never should have slept with him. How could I have been so stupid? And then I was overcome with rage towards him, disappointment in myself, and that anxiety of thinking that one day all of Barcelona might know that, down there, I was too wet.

TEN

I was nineteen and a soulless guy had just dumped me because I didn't eat and because I was too wet down there. For days I had been distraught about being at the farmhouse with my whole family, trapped in their rhythms, their long lunches, their suffocating fat bodies, and so I made lists, lists and more lists. Finally, I calmed down.

My mother and all my uncles and aunts were going out of town for a few weeks to visit a cousin who had just taken her vows as a nun and I only had to put up with five days, five days and that was it, I would have the house to myself for all of August. After that I would return to Barcelona and I could put myself back together. That image of the future relaxed me. Thinking that I would have time to compensate, I stopped controlling what I ate. I stopped vomiting and jogging until I was dizzy or convinced I had sweated it all out. I swallowed what was in front of me in the most natural way possible and pretended to have a terrible migraine so I could leave the table.

After Sunday, when they would leave in a ridiculous cavalcade, I would only need five days to cleanse my body of that abundance, and I'd still have ten to purify it completely. I wanted to expel what filtered into me beyond my control. Erect barriers. Keep them back. Burn fields. Strangle someone to death. But all I did was huddle in my room, my nose filled with snot and my brain swollen, picking up books that barely distracted me. Had I caused all of that? Had I asked him if we were going to play more games? Had my mother found me under that bed?

In those years my life followed a strict regime: graphs of goals, punishments, and sacrifices. I was pure discipline, constantly following a military drumbeat so as to avoid looking down, or inside, and to keep from falling. No matter how small the trauma I hadn't digested was, for me it was too big. And so I reduced my world to getting on the honor roll and weighing less than forty-two kilos. There were also sports, my mother and my Uncle Jaume, who had given my mother money to help take care of me when my father needed his income for other women. "That's what family's for," he would say every time I thanked him, and I thanked him often.

The day before their trip the nerves in my head were so taut that I moved slowly to keep them from snapping, only feeling good in bed and in the dark. I already had an ice pack on my forehead and was using my last bit of strength to close my eyes when my mother came into my room to tell me that my beloved uncle had had a very bad night. They were taking him to the hospital and postponing their trip for the time being. "There's food in the kitchen," she said. "We'll be back late." And she left without closing the door.

The darkness devoured me. An impossible future seized me. Every day I would become more immense, more fat, more wet, more of a slut and more of a dumbbell, and that tension I felt over living, just living, would never go away. Nerves and mental exhaustion. Was that what awaited me? Nerves that took up my entire body and made my head tight, tighter and tighter, tighter and tighter, until I was numb and dizzy for days? Why was everything about me broken? I wanted to rest. To stop that anxiety, that swollen brain and the pain that would follow.

I tried making lists, lists of fears and of food, of ideas to kill the solids and liquids that invaded me, procedures for getting through the next few days, lists of people I would strangle and formulas for avoiding it, but I couldn't calm myself down. As if I'd been programmed days earlier, I rose from the bed where I was stretched out, grabbed my mother's sleeping pills and gobbled them down. Were there enough pills? At least to put an end to the immediate suffering. And to speak without having to speak.

I showered and stretched out in the bed again. After that I don't remember anything else until some fantastical creatures, singing in strange languages and knocking on doors at the town's farmhouses, woke me up. One of them came over to me and let out a very shrill little shriek that grew louder until it was extremely loud. And now my mother, who leaned over me and called out to someone. She came and went, she never shut up, she sat me up, she wanted to lift me, make me vomit, find out what I'd taken. "I want to sleep," I said. But she wouldn't leave me alone.

A little while later my uncles and aunts arrived and I wanted to get up to see what Jaume was doing, and I thought I had, but I only thought I had. It was he who came over to me and put his big hand on my forehead while my mother said in that sweet voice she used with the poorest immigrants: "She is in such a rush to get better that today she took all my pills."

If I wanted to speak, I would have to find the strength all on my own, because my family would do anything and everything to not have to listen to me.

If I wasn't half-drunk, I would never have told her about that last episode, because not even Robert knew about it. Who would marry someone who prefers to cease to exist rather than confront her own family? But she had lived through worse things, and besides there was that wine, and the rancid air of that restaurant, where it seemed that everyone was hiding some abuse or a hanged brother.

"And why didn't you tell the truth instead of not eating?"

"When you put it like that," I said, bursting into laughter, "you're right. It seems like the more intuitive solution. But it took me years to come to that conclusion. Besides, remember that they were paying for me to go to a good school. And a homeopath!"

"Damn," she blurted out. "To fix what they'd broken in you."

I hadn't been expecting any revelation from the ill-fated girl. And yet I had never thought about it that way. I suppose that I had so ingrained the idea that my muddled head was all my fault, that I would have suffered the same way, been weighed down with the same problems, in any other place.

We finished off the bottle of wine and for the first time in two hours she stood up. The restaurant had gradually emptied and filled up again, emptied and filled, but the men at the tables always seemed like the same ones. She came back with two lemon ice creams served in their peel, the kind we used to have at school at least twenty years ago, and some strange liqueur.

"You really made him diet, that guy at university?"

"Honest. I would make huge scenes when he ate too much. And he wasn't fat at all, but I was convinced he was a total pig and I would cry and say I didn't want to sleep with him because his spare tyre would jiggle. He killed himself exercising. I even gave him a purifying treatment: ten days of a syrup he had to drink with water and lemon. It was most effective! But not a very balanced diet: maple syrup for breakfast, lunch, and dinner. And then I would send him off to ride an exercise bike."

She laughed so hard she cried fat tears. She said that she made her first and only boyfriend hang off highway overpasses to spray-paint declarations of love, because all devotion and affection seemed like too little to her, until one day he almost died. Then she started to worry that he'd end up in a wheelchair, because she really loved him a lot, despite not being entirely sure that he loved her, and she made him come to live there at the family inn, and they moved into her parents' old bedroom.

"Wasn't it hard for you to live above the restaurant after your brother killed himself?"

"Of course. But I hadn't done anything, and I didn't feel like letting them push me out of my own house. It seemed unfair, you know? My place is here."

I was shocked. I suppose they had pushed me out of my house. Away from the plain and its accent I loved best, away from so many words that would die with our grandparents; away from the children of those farmhouses, who weren't as idiotic as they were at school; away from my other uncles and aunts, who would never know what I carried inside. I let them all think that I was a strange girl, crazy like my father and my grandmother. Maybe a prude who was embarrassed by the countryside and the farms. No one had said: "Don't ever come back." But I had stopped going, especially after I met Robert. And now I only occasionally came up to visit my mother, like I'd done that very afternoon, to make sure that she seemed to be doing okay, just as she'd done with me for so many years.

"Well, I didn't know how to stay in my place," I said.

"Maybe it wasn't your place," she said, scraping up the last bit of lemon ice cream, and for the first time all afternoon she looked at me with pity in her eyes. "And how did you get away?"

How could I explain it? I tried when I finished high school, but I wasn't brave enough and it took me another decade. Especially because my mother never left that farmhouse. In fact, the older she got and the more dead siblings and relatives she accumulated, the more days she spent there. She buried herself there so she could continue to be a victim. And when she used that pathetic little birdie voice to say I didn't visit her often enough and I'd abandoned her after everything she'd done for me, and worst of all in those circumstances, she left me reeling. I was the most important thing in her life, the only thing that gave meaning to the torture that was my father, about whom she told me increasingly sad and sadistic stories. And that was how I repaid her?

That was how I repaid her because the more distance I put between me and that house and the cold tile on my butt—even though it gnawed at me to flee without blowing it all up—the less rage I felt for her and for myself. The more I was able to sleep and to focus, the less fear and disgust I felt about my body. When I met Robert I had already done a lot of work. If not, it would've been a failure like so many other times.

"But I'm not like you," I told her, quite drunk from that liqueur. "It's not that I planned it like this, but really what I did was swap one family for another."

There was a strange silence. Many men had already left the restaurant and all that was heard was the sound of plates and cups behind the bar.

"I must be afraid of being alone in the world."

"Just like everybody else," she said, and filled my glass with water. "You think there is anyone who can live without a net?"

ELEVEN

They cooked all day long to make me happy, because my mother only had one daughter and everyone knows you only turn twenty once. I was thrilled because I had discovered a new chemical laxative that the pharmacist told me was very efficient, much more so than the seaweed and pills I'd been taking.

It was a special one-of-a-kind day and relatives and friends were coming to celebrate, so an enormous meal was planned. I calculated that I should take a quarter bottle of laxative between the appetizers and the main course, and another quarter bottle after dessert, making a generous calculation and erring on the side of excess. Not because I didn't trust the pharmacist but because it was the first time I'd decided not to vomit and I wanted to make sure the new method would leave me clean on the inside.

Initially quite relaxed about the whole thing because the laxative was transparent, I didn't think I'd have any problem pulling it out of my pocket and pouring it into a cup when the time came. But my mother didn't take her eyes off me. She was sitting two seats down beside Cecília, the woman who used to let me stay at her house when I was little and who'd traveled a long way to be at that meal.

My mother was being so watchful that I decided it would be best to not do anything funny until the desserts were served, when I would go to the kitchen for the smaller plates and could empty out the bottle. But as the meal progressed I got more and more anxious, because we were eating too much and my plan to split the laxative into two doses had failed.

It wasn't an arbitrary plan. By that point I had some fairly elaborate theories on the digestive system and complete awareness of any food sedimentation inside of me. But I was afraid that if I slugged down the laxative after dessert it would be too late, and that I would have already filtered all the food into my blood and wouldn't be able to expel it.

In the end I managed to escape to the kitchen before dessert.

Once there, led by scientific instinct and my anxiousness to get out everything that was taking root inside me, I made up my mind. I squeezed the entire bottle of laxative tightly so I could drink it in one gulp without mixing it with anything. It was like kissing a test tube.

I went back to the table and when we toasted perhaps half an hour later, all the forces in the universe came together in my stomach. People came over to wish me a happy birthday and I slipped into an inner black hole that led me far away from both my body and them. My sphincter gaped open mercilessly.

Suddenly all the lights went out, the voices stopped and, just as I was convinced I was delirious and about to fall flat on the floor, my mother appeared with a cake so I could blow out the candles. Finding the necessary breath was the most difficult test of physical strength I've ever faced and when the lights came back on they found me so white and trembling that they sat me down on the sofa.

"Did you take my sleeping pills?" my mother asked me. I shook my head and Cecília believed me. No, of course not, it was just the excitement of the day, and with so many people paying me so much attention I'd gotten flustered.

"You're not pregnant, are you?" she then asked, and I thought that I'd rather drink bleach than blow up with a baby planted by that obese boy from the big city who knew too many things about me. No, I wasn't pregnant. I'd have to really love a man to let him distend my body with his child.

My stomach hurt, but thinking that I would soon be able to empty it and that the new laxative would be effective for even more fatty and lard-filled evenings than that one, I gradually came round and the guests slowly returned to their conversations. They were already asking who wanted coffee, and I didn't have long to wait before I could say goodbye.

"Don't you want to try the cake?" asked my mother, and she sat me at the table. "Come on, I made it just for you. And it'll raise your blood sugar."

I couldn't finish it. A huge burning in my stomach and an evil twist of my intestines had me squirming. I let out elephant farts. And, disproportionately dizzy, quite unlike the dizziness I felt when I was hungry, I leaned over and fell to the floor.

The hot weight in my pants made me stand up suddenly. Laughing from the infernal pressure of many eyes staring at me, I said I was very tired, very happy to see everyone but very tired, and that I needed to rest. Just as I was thinking my politeness would save me, because politeness had always worked as a distraction, my mother got up from the table and followed me to the bathroom.

"Before lunch you were so happy that I wondered if you had something up your sleeve," she said. "And now this fainting. Never a day's rest with you, Claustre…"

I got rid of her with a macabre joke, the kind that leave her side-lined, and I was finally able to lock myself in my childhood bedroom. Once alone, I rushed to find something I could pour the contents of my pants into. Why hadn't I planned it earlier and left a cereal bowl under the bed? I guess I didn't know the effect the laxative would have and I thought that at some point I would be able to get to the bathroom alone.

Searching in the dark for something I could use, all I found was a shoe box. I wanted to line it with plastic so it wouldn't leak, but I didn't have time. I released a thick, smelly torrent that, to my horror, just kept coming. The box was getting all soft and it wouldn't hold up much longer.

There, squatting in the dark over a shoe box, with laughter and voices in the background still toasting my health and the great future ahead of me, I entered another dimension. Because when the smelly paste stopped, water started coming out and even after that I was still excreting. My entire body gave every sign of emptying, my entire self struggled to void itself, I was even making the belligerent sounds of excretion, but nothing was coming out, there was nothing that could come out. I howled hysterically and involuntarily.

"My God, why have you forsaken me?" I prayed. And what a pathetic death, if this was how it all ended, curled over, crouching in the dark, shitting amid shabby toys. I was sweating like a pig but shivering with cold, sobbing and sobbing over the box. After a long while of excreting nothing, my sphincter was so dilated that all the peace in the universe entered my body. Imagining an immense man hugging me and taking me to a beautiful place where I was loved, I was then jolted by another cramp, much stronger than the others, that suddenly put me in my place: I was a pathetic twenty-year-old woman who lied to everyone every day and gave nothing to the world. If only I were fifteen so I could justify it! But I was already twenty. Twenty! When everyone else was starting to work on big projects, like a prestigious job, a doctoral thesis or a family, I was dehydrating myself out my asshole into a shoe box.

"Somebody get me out of here," I begged, and I realized I hadn't made a wish when I blew out the candles. Whatever. There was nowhere I could go. Hell was inside me.

TWELVE

We were on our way to our college graduation party when I shat myself inside a car that belonged to one of my classmates. During that period, I would gorge on laxatives because I could no longer go days without eating but I also couldn't stand the feeling of having anything inside my body. And though I was a professional, and in general controlled the timing to avoid being around people when the laxatives kicked in, sometimes I still got unexpected results. Then I would twist from the stomach pain and struggle to keep anyone else from noticing as, unable to get to the bathroom in time, I shit myself.

When we parked and I saw the long line to get into the venue, I thought: you're in big trouble now. I always carried towels and a fresh pair of panties in my bag so I could clean myself up, but it would be quite a while before we could get in. I was wearing a brownish dress but it was very thin, so I was worried the liquid would trail down my leg, or go through the fabric and everyone would realize I smelled bad. And my stomach was in agony.

I'd been combining chemical laxatives with natural laxatives for two years at that point, and when they stopped working for me, I would use enemas. Often, all that came out was a yellowish gelatin and I would think: One of these days you're going to kill yourself, you'll destroy your intestine or a kidney. But I thought about it fleetingly, not stopping to really ponder it, because I suppose if I did then I would've had to ask myself why I was doing all that. And the truth is I didn't know. I needed to expel anything that entered my body and, if I could have, I would've expelled myself too. The laxatives were painful but cleaner than vomiting, and I had already exhausted that alternative by damaging my throat.

On that June night, my fellow graduates, drunk, hot and euphoric, were deep in discussion, not knowing they'd spend the next three years as secretaries or school lunchroom monitors, cutting up pork cordon bleu into bite-sized pieces. We'd brought supermarket whisky for the wait and I was more or less taking part in the conversation between the freshly-minted communication professionals and translators. But after ten minutes I could no longer stifle my churning intestines and felt the runs coming on. I had to think out my plan carefully, since any sudden movement—and taking long strides to make a quick exit was a sudden movement—could break me and leave me dazed and shitty in front of all those well bred kids. Eventually deciding to go back to the parking lot, I said I'd left my wallet in the car and went to look for a secluded spot where I could empty my guts, clean the gelatin off and change my panties.

I moved slowly, clenching my butt cheeks, taking short steps through all my classmates. When I finally turned the corner leading to the parking lot, my heart sank: the line of cars snaked far into the distance. There was no way I could make it. And I couldn't just squat near a car because none of them were even half shrouded in darkness: the whole area was filled with halogen spotlights and young people. Desperate, I saw—I don't know how, because I hadn't noticed it on the way in—a smaller, less crowded entrance into the club, watched over by two security guards. I practically dragged myself there, very low on both time and strength, contorting from the stomach pain, and about to release a new stream of diarrhea.

"No admittance, Miss," they informed me in Spanish.

"I need to use the bathroom. It's an emergency."

"I'm sorry, but unless you have a VIP pass, I can't let you through."

And faced with that impassive wall, I fell to the ground and started to cry. At first, the guard must have thought I was drunk, because he didn't bat an eyelid. The people passing by avoided me. Some of them stepped on me. "Can't you move to one side?" they asked. I don't know how long I was there before the guard kneeled beside me and said: "If you aren't feeling well, why don't you go home?" I never would have told him that it was my college graduation party and the whole department was there, that I had been studying like a fiend for four years to keep my scholarship and that, above all else, I needed to pretend that everything was fine and that I was normal. At that point, aged twenty-three, I had managed to achieve exactly the same things I would have if I hadn't had all that stuff going on in my body and head.

"Please, I need to go to the bathroom," I begged him again. The guard, about whom I can only remember small eyes and Herculean arms, snorted and went over to speak with his partner. Then he took me by the arm and led me inside as if I were disabled. We went through a vestibule where women were leaving their handbags and men their summer jackets. We crossed through a room where everyone was in black tie and finally, with me leaning on him, hanging off that arm almost as if it were a branch, we reached the bathrooms.

Sitting on the toilet staring at those poop-filled panties made me feel sorry for myself. I didn't remember feeling that sad since the day I'd vomited in the shower and slipped on it, destroyed by two weeks of antibiotics I'd taken for tonsilitis, disappointed because I'd puked up what was supposed to help me get better, anxious because at my mother's apartment there were no latches on the doors and the shower was the only place I could think of to vomit in. I could draw a map of the country's toilets: toilets in bars, libraries, schools, foul gas stations, small town cafés, toilets where I've done a thousand and one appalling things and afterwards just wanted to die.

I had incorporated these voluntary tortures into my daily routine since I was sixteen. Controlling everything I ate was the only way I could control my anxiety. And I didn't know exactly where my anxiety stemmed from. It was like constantly living with panic despite there being no danger in sight. When I was younger, I thought the defect was my body, it both grossing me out and frightening me. But then I saw that it was my soul, which couldn't bear the feelings and turned everything into constant anxiety with varying degrees of pain. An anxiety—I believed until very recently—that was indistinguishable from, and defined, me. They had taken me to psychologists, psychiatrists, and homeopaths. Nothing. I was just like that, they said. Like my grandparents and my parents: prone to nervousness, made of cracks, unable to deal with the big situations. Breaking that chain of inner collapse was the driving force in my life.

That night, when I left the bathroom, I called a classmate to ask her to come and get the keys to the car, saying that something at dinner hadn't sat well with me and that I needed to leave. I waited outside the nightclub, at the entrance reserved for VIPs. Sitting on a post, I started to feel sad for that large, kind guard who had dragged me to the bathroom and waited for me to change and recover a bit. Who knows where that man was from. And who knows what he'd seen before landing at the doors to that room filled with famous people and television celebrities.

The classmate I'd called wanted to wait until the taxi arrived to take me back to the monastic residency where I was living at the time. I was carried off by an old, sudden sleepiness, as always happens when I let myself go because I want to disappear. I woke up six hours later, hazy and with only a vague memory. It wasn't that I had drunk too much, but rather that for years scenes and conversations wouldn't stick in my mind, perhaps—I believed—because my brain was so malnourished.

I rushed to take off my clothes so I could wash them: the fresh panties I'd put on in the VIP bathroom were wet with yellow gelatin, but the dress I'd bought for the party was still unscathed. Considering how thin and cheap it was, it felt like a miracle. As did I. Ashamed and confused, I instinctively gave thanks to God for having saved me yet again.

THIRTEEN

I was staying in a basement in Berlin because I had to eat apples for two months. I also sold tickets in a museum and read on the banks of the River Spree. But what I really needed were the apples. I had to empty myself out from the inside, expel some pressure and eliminate the many people who would come up to me and ask me things, and I could only do that with apples and a blade from a pencil sharpener that I ran over my fingertips.

I shared the basement with two slacker Germans who watched the World Cup all day long. When they spilled beer on the floor they would wipe it up with one of the pizza boxes that formed a carpet of filth. But I liked them because I didn't really care about them and they filled the house without ever asking anything of me.

When Octavi came to visit me in early July I'd been disinfecting myself for a month. By drinking many liters of water and running kilometers every morning, I had gotten rid of the pressure inside and expelled the supplicant, sticky souls. That was why I considered his visit a reward, because I had eaten a lot of apples, I had spent enough hours alone, and I was once again master of myself and able to control the perimeter surrounding me.

"What a dank, dark shithole," said a horrified Octavi as soon as he opened the door.

"Maybe I can find you a lamp…"

"It's not that, Clau. I can't work here."

"So what do you want to do?"

"Well, I'll find a hotel. Why don't you come with me?"

I left the basement in a rage and took him to a street filled with hotels. On the way there, I let him have it. I was the love of his life and he couldn't even tolerate three days in my apartment? Why did he have to make that disgusted face? To humiliate me? To remind me that I was poorer than him? Why did I have to always be the one to adapt to his needs?

"It was really difficult for me to find three days to make this trip," he replied. "Don't turn them into a bloodbath."

Telling him to get out, that I hadn't asked him for anything, I also told him he was selfish and a cold monster and that he didn't understand the most basic human necessities. And I got so angry, so livid, that I finally turned around and left without thinking that he had the keys to my place and that the two German dudes were out celebrating some World Cup victory. When I went back, he wasn't where I'd left him with his perplexed expression and wheelie suitcases. I had no phone or money on me so I walked home and sat down on the steps to my basement apartment, trusting that he would soon realize he had my keyring and that I was stranded.

Time passed, as did a lot of drunk Germans celebrating victories, and my head was spinning because early that morning I'd had to run for ages to make up for the three days when I would probably be eating more than I should. I knew he would come, because he always came to rescue me, and in the end when he showed up he couldn't help but laugh. "What are you doing sitting there? Get up and grab a few things, let's go to the hotel."

I accepted but assumed he would want sex and so thought it better to go out for dinner first. That way I could use the exercise in bed to burn off the dinner and fall asleep with my blood and stomach clean. Besides, there was a restaurant I'd had my eye on for a long time. I'd stop in front of it and always tell myself that maybe one day, when I have some leeway because I'm feeling like my weight is really low, I could go there with Octavi. That wasn't yet the case as I didn't feel like I had my weight under control, but I was pretty convinced I could find a way to compensate and besides, I really wanted to talk to him.

We talked about the Nazis and Churchill, and we laughed about the money I'd been scammed out of online when I tried to rent a more decent apartment and about a moronic, sadistic boss Octavi had already taken down a peg or two. Everything was going well until he said: "Will you quit slicing your fingertips?"

"It's relaxing. And I don't ever ask you for anything. Why don't you shut up and leave me alone?"

Suddenly he lost it. He told me to stop saying I never ask him for anything. That love wasn't about stealing from those we care about. "Love isn't an exchange of merchandise. Why the hell do you get everything so wrong? Why can't you see?" he said. He was frightening me, raising his voice, and it was making my brain swell. "This obsession of yours with leaving, with appearing and disappearing on a whim, your obsession with protecting yourself is absurd. And it hurts me. Take life by the horns, Clau, be brave."

Was I a coward? The more he spoke, the more defeated and distanced from him I felt. Yet on the other hand, he loved me without pity and that was good for me. You can't see mental disorders, and as I never explain anything, people don't believe they exist. That's made my life complicated, it's made me seem cowardly and selfish to those who love me, and like a lunatic to most. It's placed me in grotesque, incomprehensible situations, but it's also meant that no one treats me indulgently, forcing me to be better than I can be.

That night in Berlin, Octavi and I slept together and I was able to get my blood and stomach really clean. In Barcelona, too, we spent a few more toxic years together. After that I disappeared for much longer and he fell in love with another girl. No one else had ever left such a void. Maybe because he had a very rigid, very strong, character and when he chose you he went in so deep and occupied recesses you didn't even know you had. Maybe because at the time I was very lonely. Or maybe because he always called me by different nicknames. Not being myself, or at least not being myself to him, healed a wound and opened up a different future for me.

Even now, when I'm down, I think about his horrified face when he saw that filthy basement covered in beer cans and pizza boxes. But then I think about all the time we wasted, and most of all about that space that suddenly opened up because we didn't really understand each other, and the whole thing makes me sad. I didn't want to ask him for anything so I wouldn't have to give it back, so I wouldn't have to give anything to him when he asked for it. I was still paying for the

65

hot meals and the expensive school from when I was a little girl. And, besides, I needed all my strength to keep running away.

FOURTEEN

During those years we spent a lot of evenings in a ramshackle bar where they recited depressing poetry. I'd finished college two years before but had only been able to string together poorly paid assignments and obscure scams. Alternating starving with stuffing myself followed by laxatives, I often visited an ecumenical community in the Garraf. By night I would go out with Eduard, a brilliant, promiscuous friend with whom I'd formed a sort of family, united by sincere grief and macabre euphoria in the face of the absurdity and sordidness we saw everywhere.

I remember it was May and that we were waiting for a composer from Besalú who was working part-time as a rookie dealer. Acting as our supplier, over the months we'd adopted him as one of our own; he lacked any sexual instinct and so his presence made everything more relaxed, and he was self-deprecating in a very sweet, very dignified way. The three of us had formed a bond and were fixtures in that den of slackers, bookworms, and the occasional prostitute.

The rookie dealer arrived around ten thirty with a couple of friends whom I'd seen before in his huge, desolate apartment. Drinking, we polished off what he'd brought over, and I sat next to one of the friends. Andreu was a tall, elegant guy who held a menial position at an important publishing house, trusting he'd someday be promoted.

"Thou shalt not do drugs," he said when it was my turn, like a commandment, as if the Holy Spirit had anything to do with cocaine. He was clearly an intelligent and cultured young man, but he squandered it on irony and the need to show off. During the two hours we sat at the bar he couldn't stop playing with words and making jokes whenever possible. Such simple vanity was fairly easy for me to control and lead anywhere I wanted to. It wasn't that I liked him, he actually rubbed me the wrong way because of his 'wit' and the way he allowed himself to be humiliated by his slave-driving boss, but I was in the mood to defeat someone, in the mood for violence.

I didn't think twice when he said I should come to his place. I felt bad for Octavi, whom I'd been seeing for years, but our erratic history made me anxious and I didn't know how to end it or move it in a better direction for both of us. And out of a deep-seated anger, the same old anxiety and absurdity of my directionless life, I made a habit of quick sex with men I barely knew. Andreu is one of the first strangers I remember, when sex still recharged me and brought me back to the world.

Since he lived with his parents, he asked me not to make noise. I was expecting a discreet night, but once we were in bed he came to life, transforming into something more than a publishing flunky, and at some point he even tried to slip it in my ass. Not having any experience with that, I got scared. Besides, the enemas had left my large intestine very inflamed. I told him no way, that we barely knew each other, and he looked at me as if I weren't all there. "It's not like we knew each other enough to end up where we've ended up," he replied.

He was totally right about that, but at the time I didn't have the heart to explain to him that we each choose our line in the sand and, in fact, that was one of the most important decisions we make in life. It wasn't the moment for profound reflections and, wanting to lose myself in action, I sought out his hairless body which made me feel both apprehensive and a bit sad.

When I left his place a few hours later I called Eduard, who was at home and awake, listening to some new songs our asexual dealer had composed. He made space for me on his sofa and we laughed like lunatics over the anal scene. "You have the habits of a nun," he said, knowing nothing about my dances with the colon and rectum. And then we talked about the anus, about its generosity, and about the seventy-year-old antifascists who suck the life out of people like Andreu, those patient flunkies we would never be. I mentioned that I might move abroad at the end of the year as it had been a while since I'd traveled. We had a friend living in Aberdeen who would probably be an anchor for me while I got on my feet. I'd figure something out.

"I'll visit you," he said.

"No, you won't," I pre-empted. He kind of laughed and refilled his glass, directing an imaginary orchestra.

"Probably not."

If only he could one day imagine a job, a wife, some kids, something he'd created, I thought. And I fell asleep very soon after that, with my trip and my new life in my head, the strings playing in the background and the clear feeling I'd been hoping for, of beginning to shed an encumbrance.

FIFTEEN

The year I returned to Catalonia was the longest one ever. That time in Aberdeen had been a mirage. Abroad… abroad is always a dead front. We can only wage war from our parents' house.

I had grown strong far from home. I'd gained distance and that helps you comprehend what keeps you in thrall and is slowly eating away at you. But comprehension is not enough. My fears were still there, exactly where I'd left them two years earlier.

As soon as I landed I found out that Octavi, my on-again, off-again boyfriend over the last eight years, had fled. He'd waited to tell me in person, to shape my amorphous, restless interior to the very end, but he was already living with a woman and didn't want us to see each other anymore. I was in pure despair. I can see now that two berserk people can't calm each other down and hold each other up, and I have to thank him for not letting himself be mistreated again. But those years we spent hurting each other had been the only constant source of love in my life, the night light we leave on to stave off fear of the dark. And now it was over. Everything was pitch black and the earth was swallowing me up.

It was only thanks to a young dwarf nun I had gone to college with that I started to teach English at a language school in a poor neighborhood. I had eight illiterate students whose studies were subsidized by the state. Every once in a while, I would also get some interesting assignment: an interpreting gig, a novel to translate. I should have been able to find my way again, keep working until I was afloat, but over those months I'd lost the instinct for life that they'd blessed me with one August afternoon at my baptism, when my mother alone held me up over the baptismal font because at the last minute my father had chosen to go to the bar instead, as she used to like to tell me.

You can shit in all sorts of places, keep hysteric watch over every inch around you, flagellate yourself with vomit and sex, and still ooze a primitive desire for life. What would have become of me without the macabre, tender laugh that overtook me, gratuitously and at the wrong time?

Now it had evaporated. And all I could do was take the bus, close my eyes over the fifty-minute trip and repeat grammar and expressions in front of the eight sacrificial lambs that poverty was sending north for work. I didn't have that constant anxiety, I didn't punish myself the way I used to. I'd found a miserable studio to live in and I could control my mother when she wanted to devour me, but I was living somewhat underground, sustained by habits, and very far from everything.

I fulfilled my duties with grammar and expressions for more than five months, until one Wednesday in November. I had gotten up, showered, and dressed myself as best I could. But when I was doing my hair I found a clump of it in my hand and I had to urgently sit down on the floor, faced by a very old pain. I couldn't stand up. The universe was crushing me and weighing me down. I couldn't stop crying. I didn't know where my soul was and my body was left there, uninhabited.

The following week, with a sensation of total defeat, I went to see a doctor of my own volition for the first time in my life. I wanted to know if I had any mechanical defect. Where that underground world had come from, a world where everything was slow, dense, gigantic. Why after everything—when there was no longer any real threat because I didn't make myself vulnerable, when I no longer stank or saw myself as fat or dumb because I didn't look at myself—was I shattering, out of joint and without honor? I had to confront it. But how can you confront anything when your soul is detached like a dead person?

"You don't have anxiety because you are deeply depressed," a short round woman named Gabriela informed me. I liked her because she was foreign and spoke such rudimentary Catalan that she made it easy to understand the mental gobbledygook. "Anxiety is excessive energy in the nervous system. You've been through a lot of tension and fear, and your depression now is like a hangover."

A hangover. A hangover after what party, Lord? "You don't have any 'mechanical defect'," she said, chuckling, "but your brain has suffered for many years and is addicted to that feeling. We have to reprogram you. It will take a long time. I want you to be clear on that before we get started."

Taking a person apart and putting her back together. I didn't believe in getting to the root of my problems. I didn't even believe problems had roots. And how would knowing the origin fix anything? There's nothing deep down. You have to run away because even if you learn privileged information about life and the world it does you no good as it undermines your vitality and sinks you into the muck. I didn't want to take a stroll through my inner catacombs. But Gabriela insisted on an atavistic feeling of vulnerability, on the first bonds of chaos and emotional extorsion, and on all that stuff, which was actually called the sexual abuse of a little girl. She said I could cover it up all I wanted, as everyone had tried to do, but it wouldn't disappear. I suppose she was right. I suppose that I was still trapped between that large, immense body and the wall of the room where I played with puppets.

"Did you know that a third of the young women who purge and self-harm are hiding some type of sexual abuse?" No, I didn't know that. And at some other point in my life I would have said: "Leave me alone, lady. And fuck off with your bullshit psychology; I don't ask anybody for anything and, despite the anxiety, I've done okay for myself." But I had exhausted all my energy, even the energy I needed to run away, and I had to get out of that subterranean world and at least recover my impulse to lift myself up over the excrement and imagine another life.

What other option did I have besides digging up all that stuff I didn't even want to think about? Tolerating that defect in all its possible metamorphoses because suffering was just a part of life? Asking for pills to escape the immediate underworld because there are only temporary solutions? I didn't want to vomit up what someone who loves me cooked for me. I wasn't going to fornicate in bars in the city with men I find disgusting and pitiful. I didn't want to drink until my liver exploded either, or suffocate the people who'd chosen me. Over time I'd grown bored of lying and by that point it provoked an instinctive, almost physical, repulsion in me. I didn't want to let myself go. What's more, I felt like I'd already lived an entire century, but I had only just turned twenty-seven.

SIXTEEN

I met her at a bar on the Passatge Calders, a bar with immense doors that, when open, turned the whole place into a continuation of the street. She was sitting on a stool, alone at a table that could have held three or four people. Since the other tables were full and I didn't want to sit at the bar—that would've meant I'd have my back to people and they could have stabbed me or strangled me with some belt or leash—I sat down with her. She was tall like me, very thin like me, and had curly blonde hair like me. Her large black eyes reminded me of mine. But her teeth were larger and whiter, and less crooked, and that made her different, and when she laughed and said: "I'm Leonora and I'm Uruguayan," that was it.

She'd studied journalism but had worked as a photographer, making handmade jewelry, and teaching pottery classes to kids. Now she danced on the street. Or not exactly. She would dance with no script and occasionally twist herself around a fence or a streetlight and make a human sculpture. She showed me some photographs of her art, which she'd been practicing for the last year in Barcelona, but before that in São Paulo, Buenos Aires, and Berlin. Leonora leaping and prancing in the Marco Zero. Leonora stretched out in the Plaza de Mayo with a bloody sheet on her stomach. Leonora hanging from the Bismarck Memorial in the Tiergarten emulating a rifle or a snake —or was it a scarf?

I couldn't stand people wasting their money getting a degree and then not using it, and I didn't like shirkers who switched jobs all the time; you never knew exactly what they knew how to do, except travel a lot more than you with money they'd leeched from some strange organization or another. We've ruined everything, I thought. Christianity, the family, social mobility. We should at least preserve the professions. A society's degree of civilization can be measured by the number of professions it still has. I was utterly convinced of that. But even though Leonora's patchwork job trajectory drove me nuts,

I didn't hate her urban sculpture. And I definitely didn't hate the way she told me about it, with her big, white, straight teeth, and her breasts, smaller than mine but rounder and firmer.

We had one drink after another and left the bar at two-thirty. I lived two streets above the Passatge Calders and offered to walk her to the Gran Via so she could catch a cab. She said: "No, no way," that she would walk me to my apartment. I accepted in exchange for her letting me call a taxi to pick her up in front of my house. It was too late to walk alone. We sat in the doorway and I started talking about Werther, which is what I always do when I'm feeling terribly embarrassed and I don't want to talk about politics or religion because I don't think the other person and I would see eye to eye. She would laugh a bit, then be silent for a bit, then look out into the distance, then stare into my eyes from very close up. I didn't know if she wanted me to get closer, and I felt the way good men must feel in such circumstances. I wanted to get her into my bed, but without offending her. I didn't want to overstep or understep her boundaries. I wanted to do exactly what she was hoping I would do.

In the bar she had told me about a couple of long-term girlfriends she'd had. So she had real experience. I didn't have much, with men or women, because with men I had problems with constancy in the bedroom and with women I never dared to tell them what was going on with me. It wasn't easy to explain in detail without getting punched in the face. I was a woman who also liked women but who had never been attracted to a lesbian because all the ones I knew seemed too masculine. I thought about how I could tell her something so terrible without offending her. She had started being with women as a teenager, so she was as lesbian as I was short and bow-legged and from Lleida. In that moment I realized, with all the sadness in the world, that all those grants that allowed her to dance around the world probably came from research groups on art and gender.

The conversation turned to my studio. If I lived alone, how great it is to be alone, how hard it is to live with a partner. I said that I wouldn't know because I had never lived with any of my boyfriends and then, I don't even know how, maybe because I was drunk, or maybe because when we need to say something we'll take advantage of any slight opening to let it out, I found myself explaining the whole truth to her. I was expecting a terrible reaction, but she didn't even blink.

"And you see yourself as feminine?" she asked me, laughing with obvious amusement.

I had never really pondered that question. I was thin, I didn't have curves or much chest, but my features, gestures, voice and extremities were all very delicate. I said that yes, I thought I was feminine, and I showed her my hands and feet, with their twenty svelte fingers and toes, as conclusive evidence.

"And what does feminine mean?" she continued, with a bit of malice.

Right then I thought she was about to hammer me with gender theory and my heart sank because that would have meant the end of our conversation. It had been a long time since I'd spoken so frankly with anyone. She was clever, expressed herself in interesting combinations of words, and wasn't angry at the world. And to tell the truth, what had distanced me from the lesbians I'd met wasn't their appearance, not by far, but rather the doctrine I would have had to swallow before going to bed with them.

I answered that, to me, being feminine meant being able to pass for a female character in a Jane Austen novel. She laughed at my silly comment and I laughed too, partly because she was laughing, and partly out of nervousness and my need for warmth. Then she kissed me. I couldn't kiss her back because my tongue wasn't working and so I stuck it out and told her it was dead, that I had a dead tongue that hadn't shown any signs of life in years, dead as a doornail. She laughed as I continued with part of my tongue sticking out, knowing as I did that she would tell me not to worry, that she would bring it back to life. And that is exactly what she told me.

Then everything happened very quickly and I didn't feel like myself. I froze up and started to cry three times, and eventually I licked her as she'd never been licked in her entire dissolute life as an itinerant artist. Leonora surging over my bed was the best human sculpture I'd ever seen, although ten hours earlier I wasn't even aware of the discipline. She was elastic, delicate; she did sweat, but pleasantly. That the dirtiest sex could be so clean—that was something I wasn't expecting.

It was almost six, my whole body ached, and I begged her for a truce. My previous, relatively uninspired sexual experiences were a joke compared to that night. Leonora ran a hand through my hair and laughed long and hard. I heard her laughing as she walked calmly to the kitchen to look for something to eat, as if she did that every morning, as if we'd bought that apartment together. Sitting at the foot of the bed, fishing cereal out of a mug, one curl wet with milk, she told me, as if in passing, "You know what your problem is?" My eyes begged her not to continue. "You're a man in a woman's body."

A man in a woman's body. Her declaration left me in an unparalleled state of shock. Impossible. I didn't feel like a man. Sure, I wasn't very vain and I had a protective instinct. And I did value my freedom above all else. It was true that I had a tendency to show off my talent and even display a certain cruelty in return for applause. It was also true that I didn't make sacrifices for anyone except myself. But that's no proof of some genital or mental mix-up, or whatever. It only meant I was low-maintenance. I don't have a father or brothers and I've always taken care of my mother as if I were the real man she needed. I have some female friends who aren't self-reliant, and my role has always been to put some order into their sentimental muddles. I like order, discipline, and preparation. Emotions and the body provoke an old shame that paralyzes me, and if the feelings are too intense, they sometimes make me vomit. But that doesn't make me a man. It makes me a woman who has to run to the toilet and puke when she sees a dramatic film or somehow finds herself at a poetry recital.

I didn't know how to respond to Leonora's comment and we fell silent for quite some time. She continued fishing out cereal, more pensively now. After a while, she started to get dressed and look for her bag, preparing to leave. Without my asking her anything, she told me she'd rather not sleep over because she gets hot so she always tries to sleep alone. And she wanted to wake up at home and get straight to work tomorrow. When she said that, tears almost fell from my eyes. I had found the perfect person for me. Her name was Leonora, she was Uruguayan, and she made human sculptures. It wasn't the life I'd been imagining, I didn't know how I would introduce her to my mother, I had no idea if we would adopt a Russian child or if she'd want to get pregnant, but that woman suited me. She wouldn't invade me. She had sweet sweat, a sense of humor, and she could see inside me without being shocked or moralizing.

She wrote her phone number down on a paper towel, kissed my hair and closed the door with a bang. I waited a few days before calling her, so I wouldn't overwhelm her and because I too wanted some time to digest what had happened. How had a Guarani artist and complete stranger made me feel I could trust her? Because she looked like me? Why did things I hated in other people seem fine when it came to her? Because she was a lesbian who didn't lecture me or destroy her looks on purpose? Was I sprung on a liberated Latin American version of myself?

It all seemed so terrible that I decided to call her so we could discuss it calmly and sleep together again. And that was how I was planning on putting it to her, since I could tell her anything. But the person on the other end of the line was a man from Arbeca—Arbeca, Lleida—who didn't know anyone named Leonora. I tried dialing various numbers, combining the numbers she'd written down, even swapping them out for similar-looking digits, in case she'd made a mistake. Because she'd been tired or hungover or because of the impact of having met the mother of her children in those circumstances, because surely starting a family would have repercussions for her life as a globetrotting artist.

There was nothing more I could do. There was no way I could get in touch with her and I spent a few weeks in anguish, searching for her in every possible place: curled up around the legs of a bench, twisted on a fence, hanging from iron rails, at the bar on Passatge Calders. Barcelona has a thousand opportunities for human sculptures so she would surely be here for a while and I'd find her, I thought. But I didn't and gradually, without even realizing it, I stopped searching for her.

When I think about it, years later, it produces a painful, oneiric feeling, like almost everything in my life. Maybe I should hold a grudge against her. It's not right, coming into people's apartments and bodies like that, ripping out their most intimate secrets and then skipping town with no warning. But how could I blame her for anything? She shook me up without breaking me. And it is very, very strange for someone to be really able to see us without eventually using it to their advantage. I had done the right thing, seizing the moment. Who knows if I'll ever have that chance again.

SEVENTEEN

She had a luminous, round face, a heart of gold, and she eyed us from a wooden frame placed on the dresser and the corkboard hung on the wall, elbowing out from amid the children's drawings. I found her pleasant and had nothing to reproach her for, but I didn't like her watching over us. I wanted to sleep with my boyfriend, who'd I'd already been with for six months, and I couldn't do it because she was staring into my eyes.

She'd been dead for four years, but Pau still had the house filled with images of her. "It's for the twins," he would say. "So their mother is always around."

At first I didn't want to go there. But what could I do? It was his house, and he had to be a father, the twins needed him, and if I wanted to see him often, as I believed at the time couples should do, I had no choice but to go there and act as if nothing was wrong.

I spread out in that house the way I always spread out. In the room where they kept the toys and the ironing board, I set up a desk, some shelves for books and dictionaries, my computer, printer, and a chair I'd splurged on because I'd suddenly wanted to take care of myself and it seemed like investing in a chair I couldn't afford would compensate for all the horrific things I'd self-inflicted. I had everything I needed. But couldn't get used to the dead woman. To her constant presence on the fridge, on the furniture in the dining room, on the kids' closets, on the dresser.

I couldn't stand that she had such a pleasant appearance, that she was so good with kids and such a kind person. You can't compete with a teacher for the love of a man as traditional as mine. A teacher is sweet, devoted, enthusiastic. She's someone who's always attentive to others. A teacher is like a nurse: a very good woman who performs as a woman, at work, everywhere.

I was always translating in the office to make money. Translating, translating, translating. And sometimes writing, to vent and 'get my ducks in a row.' I didn't like cooking and couldn't stand those family get-togethers. I also struggled to deal with the twins, especially the girl. In the evenings when the four of us would sit on the sofa, or stroll down the street, she would cling to her father as if she were afraid I was going to steal him. If he hugged me, she would start coughing or complain about some sudden pain. Kids are not good. Maybe they aren't aware of their baseness, but that's still no excuse, as I discovered when my computer broke down and we went to buy a new one.

I hadn't earned much that month, and so Pau offered to help me out. The store was full and I even ran into an acquaintance of a friend, one of those people you always tell that everything is going really well, right off the bat, when they ask how you are. And as we were waiting in line the girl starts bellowing: "You're going to pay for her computer? Why would you pay for it? Is Claustre poor? She doesn't pay any rent! She lives at our house!" It was a frightful show, and I shrank as she bellowed and bellowed that she wanted a trip to New York, that she'd wanted to buy some new device and couldn't because, according to Pau, they weren't rich and couldn't waste money on a whim. And then, looking at me, she said straight out: "We're already doing enough for her, letting her live at our house." If competing with a dead woman was difficult, competing with a dead woman and that girl was much more than I could take.

I had to rethink the entire situation, but I couldn't talk about it with him because he got scared and just kept asking me for time without ever saying exactly how much. Patience, patience, he would repeat. But patience is like a rock tied to your ankles. The patient life is a life with nothing on the horizon, shriveled. It is like a voluntary, premature death and there was already a genuine corpse in the house. There was no way I could compete.

Sick and tired of the situation, I decided to screw up my courage and speak directly with the implicated party. One day when Pau and the kids were at their grandparents' house—the parents of the dead woman, regulars in the family landscape—I gathered up all her photographs, including the wedding photos in which he was smiling ear to ear, glued to her, completely devoted to his role. I was struck to see him so present, he who always had his mind elsewhere, who lived detached from himself and distanced from the world, exactly like me. I suppose that's why we understood each other. I put all the photographs on our bed, formerly their bed. Keeping the lights dim, I stared at the dead woman and addressed her politely.

"Good evening, Dúnia," I said (her name was Dúnia). "Sorry to bother you, Dúnia. I'm Pau's new girlfriend, Claustre. Dúnia? Dúnia?" What could I do? She didn't want to communicate with me.

I kept trying for some time, until I realized I needed to improve my technique. Maybe the Internet could give me some tips for contacting the dead. It seemed ridiculous and unfair to have to ask permission to love a man I practically considered mine. But ignoring her hadn't worked and I wanted to put an end to that suffering. You can't live with the eyes of the unabsolved dead staring down on you. Besides, it had been weeks since Pau and I had slept together, creating a distance between us that I couldn't stand.

A civil servant from Oriola who moonlighted as a medium had posted her classes on the Internet. I bought everything she said to buy and waited for the right day. Not every day was a good time to contact Dúnia. She could watch me whenever she felt like it, but I had to speak with her at the proper time, using a complex calculation based on the dates of her birth and death. The dead have no other job than watching the living twenty-four hours a day, but we have to create the right situation to see them, on the proper dates to help to open up the soul and position it towards the heavens.

I grabbed a photograph where she was alone and looking very pretty, sprinkled it with donkey milk and put a few drops of patchouli oil on the bed. Following to the letter what the medium from Oriola had said, I placed a pen on a blank piece of paper. The lamp I'd wrapped in red paper added a terrible sense of foreboding to the scene.

"Helloooooo, Claaaaaustreeee, I aaam haaappy that youuu are in this houuuuse," she, through me, wrote onto the page. Taking her sweet time, Dúnia dictated to me in clear rounded handwriting. The handwriting of a good, kind teacher. I couldn't stand her.

"Let us live our lives! I order you to let us live our lives!" I had prepared an elegant and profound speech about love, freedom, and letting go, and was planning to tell her that I perfectly understood how difficult it was for her to let go of Pau and the twins, but that in my own way I loved them and would take care of them. I had a lot of nice things to tell her but ended up just screaming at her.

"Claaaaaustreeeee, reeeelaax, I am giving you all waaarmth, the waaarmth you all neeeed," she wrote in polished, perfect Catalan.

"That's not true! You're controlling me! You're always skulking around the house and I have no space to spread out! Leave!"

"You have to use thiiiiinner nooooodles in their soooooup."

This fucking teacher. She'd been spying on me and now she wanted to give me cooking lessons.

"He can make their noodles! I'm not a maid!"

"Heeeeee does maaaany thiiings foooor yoooou toooo."

That was true. But I hadn't summoned her to talk about women's liberation and its contradictions. I wanted her to disappear. Or to never have existed. I wanted her to die again. To be dead beyond dead. I wanted... what the hell did I want? To not have the feeling that if she were alive he never would've loved me. To not have the feeling that—when I lost my cool in an argument, or when I stayed up late translating and couldn't get up for breakfast with the kids the next day—they were all thinking: mom would never do that. I wanted to be free to make mistakes. Free to deal with the twins. Free to make love and not think about her corpse. I wanted not to be such a moron; I had slept with half of Barcelona and now here I was, jealous of a dead woman. I could already see that this couldn't be, that it shouldn't be, that I had to make more of an effort and be more generous. All my life I have been jealous of the love I didn't get, of the love people give to other people. And why, if I don't know what to do with it when they give it to me? I don't know if she listened to me, or if I offended her so much that she hung up and that was why she didn't dictate anything more. But the fact is, that afternoon, screaming at the woman who was still my boyfriend's wife no matter what I did, actually left me feeling relaxed, and the mood at home grew calmer.

A couple of months later the twins spent an entire Saturday moving furniture around. They wanted to move that, take this apart, paint here, hang something up over there. It was all shouting and new ideas. Pau asked me whether I'd noticed they'd been more restless lately. But I only had eyes for him, so pure of heart, with such a strong, well-formed body, so absent. And then I saw the bad, jealous little girl, as well as the dead woman, though I saw Dúnia less and less. It had been maybe six months since she'd visited my office and after our otherworldly conversation the five of us were cohabitating more comfortably. Thanks to her influence, to the loving and celestial breath that filtered into the twins' hearts, the public tantrums had stopped. As I'd been able to give her a piece of my mind, I was more relaxed, and she no longer spied on me so obsessively.

So that night, when Pau told me we should look for a new apartment with a large, private, sunny office so that I could work more comfortably, I was taken aback. I guess he was expecting me to be thrilled. Or happy. Or grateful. I suppose that taking that step would kill off the dead woman, and that all I had to do was bury her and take her place. "Wow," was all I could say. "Let's think carefully about it." And I left him on the sofa, nodding off as he watched an American primary debate. I had to revise an urgent translation but instead went to bed. Tossing and turning, I felt anxious beneath the shining eyes of the good teacher, who laughed maliciously and pushed me, now hard, toward what I had made happen.

EIGHTEEN

He was ten years older than me, but I felt so old and tired by his side. I'd been through so much anxiety and so much fear that he seemed like a man from another world. At thirty I had slept with twenty men, I'd loved five, lived in three countries and changed jobs ten times. He had only slept with one woman, his wife, a Catholic from Manresa with whom he shared two daughters and an apartment in Barcelona. And when we fell in love it was a very painful mirror.

I don't know how to explain this story without it sounding like a lesson in catechism, but for the first time in my life I didn't feel worthy of someone coming under my roof, and would have liked to erase all my previous lovers so that I could learn it all again with him for the first time.

It's not that I'd been overcome with an attack of Christian morality or that my subconscious was judging me through him: he didn't judge me. He said: "We all have our baggage and I might not love you if you didn't carry such a huge weight." And maybe he was right. But for me that love had a very special meaning, unique to date, and I couldn't find the way to set him apart from my past. What could I give him that I hadn't given a hundred times without any implication, merely thinking about how to get out unharmed?

It is hard to combine intelligence and naïveté. Robert was an intelligent man, and he knew a lot of things, but he never saw ulterior motives, the world behind the world, the lengths to which people go to get what they want. He believed he didn't see any of all that because he was a man and only women see all that. But I think he didn't see it because he was a stranger to envy and resentment and rancor and all of those feelings that make us suspicious of everything. I soon felt a cannibalistic need to protect him from all possible hurts, starting with the risks I posed.

"Remember I almost killed a poor guy by forcing him to diet. And I abandoned a widower when we were about to move in together.

Not to mention Octavi, who I'd left three times but when he fell in love with another woman, I called him threatening to leave this world behind."

Then he would look at me with those tender, gleaming eyes, both strong and fragile like so many tuberculous poets of centuries past, and say: "None of us is as bad as we think we are, ever." He was so convinced of that, and I can't tell you whether that means he was naïve or just a bit insane.

The first day we spent together I was dead tired because, attacked by nerves, I had hardly slept the night before. And he was quite hysterical and speaking confusingly, incongruously. The upstanding man with a canonical life was coming up to my apartment after lying about a work meeting. And what did he want? For us to search for the truth between us. But I wanted to tell him that I don't even know my own truth. Our truth, he said with great aplomb, and so I would have to be very honest.

The truth? I came from a place where you lied to drink on the sly, or go to the bordello, or justify some missing money at the bank, or to ask for time off work. I had grown up hearing two or three simultaneous variations on a single subject, learning that things are never what they seem. And now we had to find the truth? All I could do was try my best.

To me it was normal that we'd ended up there as we had a complete spiritual affinity. And, with the recent seminars and so many days working together, we were all worked up. It'd been years since I'd pulled an all-nighter just talking to someone without getting tired, not caring about how lucid I'd be at work the next day.

"I thought these things stopped happening once you were an adult," I said, suddenly getting sad. Then he said that it had never happened to him before.

Clearly in his case it was more understandable because after so many years of marriage he was bored and looking for a crutch. Maybe his wife had died in childbirth and now all he had left was the mother of his daughters, who didn't interest him. I must've been a distraction, an exciting, warped idea, a stimulus for his days overloaded with obligations.

"There is obviously some lying on your part," I continued, pretty much unfiltered. And then he stood up from the sofa and looked at me desperately. "You offend me," he said. He was crying. He looked at me, horrified, as if I had left him alone with that turmoil. "You offend me by calling my feelings into question," he repeated, and I clearly saw that he was absolutely nothing like the scoundrels I'd dealt with in the past, that he had a sensibility and gravity that exalted feelings and words.

"Forgive me," I said, and I stood up from the sofa too.

And then what were we to do? We didn't find the truth, but we went to bed together and then swore to never see each other again, because he couldn't envision having an affair and he didn't have the stomach to shatter a family. I accepted it serenely, without a single reproach, because I'd decided to commit the first unselfish act of my life.

"Just one thing," he wanted to ask before I closed the door on him. "When we're seventy and eighty years old, and we're both widowed, would you like to get married?"

There was no need to kill anyone or wait for some macabre gesture from the heavens, because we kept writing to each other and two weeks later we ended up back in the same place. How long had it been there? And why hadn't we ever noticed it? My hesitance, to be frank, had always been his two daughters. Maybe because I'd only sporadically had a father and it seemed like children need a permanent one: whenever a man had children I crossed him off my list. I don't know what held him back, maybe the same thing, because once he told me that he couldn't shatter a family, that if he did it would destroy his wife, who was very dependent and set limits so that she could control him better, and that he would miss his daughters. He never said that he would miss his wife, but maybe he kept that to himself so as not to hurt me, despite my telling him a thousand times to always tell me the truth about everything, that I could take it. I was sick of men you can't explain everything to because they crumble, and I didn't want him to have to take responsibility for my feelings. Not because I didn't want to be responsible for his —I loved him and I would have taken responsibility for anything of his, at any point and in any circumstances, but I didn't want his pity. When I hit rock bottom I would've accepted the pity and help of anyone, except him.

Our second encounter was no better than the previous one. Actually, when I think about it, what a pathetic image. First I was straddling him, making love to him as if that was what I'd been born to do, and next I was sobbing in the bed, curled up between the pillows, like a broke prostitute crazy for the needle. Sleeping with a family man is dissolute, I told myself. He is a cheater and repressed and is unable to have a lover without believing he's in love with her. But I felt loved like I'd never felt before, and when he left again saying we mustn't speak again for many years, I couldn't believe it.

I despaired for several weeks, with a fever and everything. I lied at work. I thought about showing up at his house and making a big scene to find out if his wife was as dependent as he claimed, or if he was pretending so he wouldn't have to leave her. It wasn't until I started to see my totally normal-sized arms and neck as wide as bollards that I realized that if I didn't think straight, in a disciplined way, that it would be the end of me.

I held up my part of the bargain, and prayed that he would hold up his, because I would no longer be able to refuse to see him if he asked. I wouldn't have been able to refuse him anything, absolutely anything, and that made me anxious and relieved, as no doubt happens to the fanatic worshipers of a bloodthirsty god. I was undone by my nerves and my stomach, I could lose my job and the roof over my head, but I would have kept seeing him if he had wanted to.

I don't know how hard it was for him to stop writing and calling me, but he didn't say another word to me until ten months later, when he wanted to have lunch, as if none of all that had happened. Having already recovered my mind, which I'd completely lost over him, I went, forgetting that losing your mind isn't like losing some money. All the ages of man coincide and they can all sprout out of season—including reckless youth.

To begin with, we controlled our conversation, maintaining quite a bit of distance from the scene. But ten minutes later I saw that he was looking at me in that way, which wasn't lust or friendship or anything I could name, and I made an insinuation. He took my idiotic insinuation and made it explicit—embarrassing me in the worst possible way.

Up until that day I had accepted his making it seem that I was the one who'd made the first move, but I was no longer willing to tolerate that. "If you want something," I said, "you have to ask me for it, because I refuse to bear the guilt, anxiety, and the sadness later." He then kissed me before saying, "Nothing ever gets past you."

Luckily, I was sitting down because it felt like the bones were fleeing my body. I wanted to touch him, to kiss him back, but all I said was: "Let's go to my place." When we left the restaurant, my feet led me home. I heard nothing, I saw nothing, I thought about nothing. We were already on my street when he stopped me abruptly and took my face in both hands. "My God," he said. And nothing more, he said nothing more, he said: "My God" and turned and ran off. I can still see him, all lanky and ungainly, with that tailored coat and his leather briefcase, trotting up Carrer Calvet, as if the Devil were at his heels.

NINETEEN

His fleeing for a third time after he was the one who called me, after I'd very nearly bled to death ten months earlier over our first two breakups, what was that? What was that? Heaven-sent revenge for the men I'd mistreated before him? A warning from God to remind me not to lower my guard?

I hadn't struggled for so many years to crumble now, and much less for a lifeless conformist like Robert. After everything, after thirty years of sleeping so badly, after deconstructing and reconstructing yourself with the damn psychologist, you cannot allow yourself to crumble over some frustrated imbecile trapped in his marriage.

But I crumbled. And I crumbled even further when I thought how, hell or high water, the shadow of that drunken failure would always be chasing me, and that if you're born broken, you die broken. For the first time I heard my mother's voice inside my own, that titchy bird-drowning-in-a-puddle voice that demands attention and doesn't know how to give it in return, and I couldn't stand it. I'd aspired to be able to enjoy life's sensual pleasures, seeing some of my projects come to fruition, even have a family and support them, and maybe I was doomed to just struggle to get by.

Fina, the dwarf nun from college who never got angry, not even the day I didn't show up for her mother's funeral because it was first thing and I couldn't get out of bed, moved into my studio for three days. She made me lunch and brought it to my bed on a tray. She sang me the songs that fill Vallbona, the Cistercian convent near my town. She read me healing passages about the meaning of sadness. And when she had to leave because the abbess was convinced that this Claustre with sudden urgent pains was some strange affair, she called me every day in secret.

When adults are dealt a blow, what do they do? Some talk to their loved ones until they can digest it. Others spend weeks dragging themselves from one bar to the next. Most of them keep quiet and rise above the silence for the rest of their lives. I descend to childish, desperate hells. The deep pits of a directionless, defenseless child. It's pathetic and disgraceful and anyway, it's incredibly hard to fathom because neither she nor the drunk ever came to my rescue, but when I fall into the pit I need an older woman, or someone with an atrophied sexual instinct, to fish me out and tell me I won't fall any deeper.

Two weeks after he fled for the third time I went back out into the world with the sensation of having spent a long time in a cave. The light falling on objects, the remarkably clear, intense sounds on the street, the feel of clothing, the food I ate at my own pace, thinking with a clear head. It was all astonishing and seemed worth experiencing.

Just a few weird days, I assured myself, and with great grief I killed Robert off in a head-on collision with a crazy Andorran who was driving in the wrong direction on the highway. I thought I was over the worst of it, after having imagined and reimagined the lethal accident, until one Friday afternoon, only five days after I'd resurfaced, he knocked on the door. He hadn't been drinking and he didn't want to leave anymore, he assured me, thinking that I wouldn't even let him in.

"Why did you deceive me, in bed?" he asked. Because it was complicated, and I didn't want to turn my body into an experiment or have him take it as a challenge. Besides, I didn't think he would realize. It was one thing to warn him about the men I had hurt and remind him that I can't be trusted. But it's quite another to stop in the middle of having sex to start explaining my problems. I'd accepted years ago that my body was a losing battle.

"This is the first freely made decision of my life," he said, wanting to make it clear. He didn't want to talk about his young daughters, or the fact that we would have no place to live, or about the money we'd have to borrow. He didn't want to talk about those things because he said that when the choice is clear, when your whole body is with you, these things have a way of working themselves out. He insisted that with truth comes strength. And besides, maybe not today, maybe not tomorrow or the day after, but in the long run living a lie does more harm.

Did he love me or the freedom I represented, even if it was so costly and we had to kill all those ghosts that kept coming back and coming back, exhausting us?

"I can't separate the two things," he said, and I appreciated that he didn't hide it from me. I was also having so much trouble believing that someone could ever love me, that I needed a blind, painful gesture like that from him.

I knew that the years would pass. Even if I had doubts, like I'd always had doubts about any love that was ever offered to me; even if deep down I thought he would rob me or take advantage of me when I relaxed and lowered my guard; and though one day I might find him repulsive and a bit pathetic, like all the men who'd come before him, I would no longer be able to separate him from the sacrifice he had made for me.

I'd been carrying a hole inside me for years. A tormenting, aggressive, entrenched distrust. And what I needed from him was complete and total self-sacrifice.

TWENTY

She woke me up discreetly, whispering my name, tapping me on the shoulder. I sat up with a start anyway. A year later, I still hadn't gotten used to having kids in the house, not even to having a man in the house. This was despite the fact that he was mine and I never locked myself in a room or thought about running away when we argued; or suddenly felt like everything was coming apart because my bond with him was breaking.

I turned on the light to look at her and she said that her father had taken her sister to school but that she'd stayed home because she wasn't feeling well.

"What's wrong?" I asked.

She got straight into bed, on the side where her father sleeps. I was shocked. Stupid kid, I told myself, involuntarily. How could she be so trusting? There was no secret compartment in her. She curled up with me and breathed laboriously. Who takes advantage of a defenseless little girl who climbs into your bed? The question came over me and filled my mind. And just as the thread tying me to the world was starting to break, Alba sat up and vomited.

I don't know if I've ever had as clear a head as I did in that moment. I still didn't know her well but I knew that years earlier she had been very sick. I didn't treat her any differently, the way everyone else did; I didn't look at her with that mix of tenderness and terror. Because it isn't the same thing to know that someone has been sick as to see them slipping away. And I guess that was why I didn't understand how weak she was. But what if this wasn't just a passing virus?

We got into the taxi like someone heading into battle, ready for whatever might be awaiting us, and on the way to the emergency room I called her father, who was just heading home. He would've come straight to the hospital, but the traffic was bumper to bumper and it was going to take a while. He didn't get upset. Robert never got upset, and that stoicism of his—which used to drive me crazy because

I took it as fear of conflict and moral superiority—had made me much more civil. When you observe how someone else behaves properly you realize, if you have half a brain, that you aren't behaving properly.

At the front desk to the emergency room sat a doltish man, his graying hair dyed black. I didn't have her documents, so everything was a problem. I found myself explaining my life, her life and, finally, after a few questions that we met with lies and avoidance, he allowed us in. Alba wasn't feeling worse and in her canary voice repeated what she'd heard her father say a hundred times: "We could save ourselves a ton of pointless explanations if we just published our story."

By that point we were over it, but the early days of our relationship had been difficult. People would volunteer their opinions about how the two girls were a burden and I was an idiot for wasting my energy and money on children who weren't my own. That hurt because it was true. At least in the beginning. I didn't want to love them. They made me feel like an idiot. I would give them everything I had, I thought, and if something ever happened to their father or me I'd never see them again, when twenty years from now they would only vaguely recall some woman they'd shared a home with. Why should I love them if they aren't mine in any way? And if one day they might disappear? Then I accepted it. I just loved them despite the circumstances and that was everything, absolutely everything, that I was feeling and could explain.

I suppose that blood ties are stronger than our ability to control them, but only love molds us deeply enough to move us to take that leap: entirely giving ourselves over, without any certainties. The love I had for him had filtered into his daughters, and I—who used to only give of myself when obliged to by the weight of debt, and only love to the point where I could still throw a few things in a suitcase and leave at any moment—discovered the closest thing to a miracle I'd ever experienced. Over time I came to understand something strange: taking care of them was like taking care of something in me. It was like pulling myself out of an old pit and protecting the big mosquito who was waiting for her father while she, who had done everything for me, including bringing me into this world with a man who didn't want children, cried on the toilet.

The fact that Robert's daughters weren't born in a cabbage patch and had a mother, a mother who wasn't me, didn't really affect me. I didn't feel jealous. I actually liked her and was interested in her recriminations of him, though I suppose it was to protect myself from my own infatuation. "I couldn't see it when we got married." I had heard that so many times, from so many men and so many women, including ones who were so smart, so cynical, who'd been around the block so many times, that I wanted to be alert. It wasn't easy, because nothing is as antithetical to love as staying on the alert, and because I, who am irascible and bitter and have every defect except envy because I get by with so little, felt pain over the years that my man had lived without me. Over his marrying, having two daughters, even the tremendously paranormal fact of the years passing for him, one after the other: it felt as if I'd been robbed. Even though I knew that five or even three years earlier he wouldn't have been able to sustain me, and that I wouldn't have been up to the task of our situation either. Up to the task, because we reach an age when we're expected to be up to the task, which first requires trusting that they won't kick you out of the house if you're seven years old and hiding under someone else's bed and they find you with no panties on.

When he arrived at the hospital that morning, lanky and rushing as always, Alba was sleeping and I was in her room reviewing all the paperwork we needed to fill out so they could run some tests on her. I hadn't even finished explaining everything when a nurse showed up to take Alba away. Since someone would have to be there all day, I decided to go back to the house to deal with some work issues, so he could have the space to organize the situation and call her mother without worrying about saying something that would hurt my feelings.

"Her father will be out in a moment and he'll be able to give you everything you need," I said in a baby bird voice to the man at the reception desk, in an attempt to make up for my irritated response earlier. "It's so agonizing..."

"Just imagine if she were yours," he answered, all chuckles. And he lowered his head to jot down what someone had just told him over the phone.

Though I used my key, it felt strange, as if someone might catch me and ask what I was doing, what I was looking for in that house. I'd driven for two hours because my mother had suffered another dizzy spell and hurt her arm when she'd lost her balance. She was still falling, or it seemed to her like she was still falling because the earth was sinking deeper and deeper with each passing moment, and she hadn't left the bed in three days.

I looked at every corner of the entryway: the long stone bench, the sprung cart that my beloved uncle had restored, the narrow stone spiral staircase with the two niches with two plaster saints with peeling paint and those metal halos I'd caught my fingers on so many times. I stopped in the hall with its black-and-white portraits: burly women, children in their Sunday best, weary men of uncertain age. Six generations accused me of being ungrateful and intolerant.

The woman who helped my mother was folding clothes in a the narrow room where I used to play with puppets more than thirty years ago. My mother was resting in her bedroom, her neck rigid, her arm bandaged, held up by a support girdle that immobilized her back.

She had grown old. Those two years since she'd stopped working had hit her hard. Selling the apartment in Lleida and moving to the farmhouse hadn't helped. After a few months of living there she started to walk like an old lady. Her black hair grew lighter and her head was covered in reddish blotches. Her scent had gotten stronger and she repeated herself more than ever.

"Where are you going dressed like that?" she said as her only greeting.

I didn't have time to defend myself. She coughed and told me that she hadn't seen me for two months but what did it matter because she was already used to it, that she understood I had a lot of work but it was as if she had no daughter. And then she started talking about my Uncle Jaume, who was going to die soon, very soon, maybe even before her. And she also told me about the letters I'd been getting there, from some library, notifying me that I'd mistakenly returned a book to them that in fact belonged to the municipal archives.

"Where's your head at, Claustre? You're just like your father, always coming back from the bar with someone else's coat. Remember that jacket from some guy named Armand?"

And she burst out laughing, laughing and laughing, laughing and laughing, until she got dizzy and had to stop. I handed her a glass of water and she took the opportunity to grab my wrist with her big freckled, liver-spotted hand that always smelled of lotion. "You look like a starving African," she murmured. And then she told me that I should stay with her, that she would feed me better, and asked after Robert in a kind, sincerely interested tone she'd never used before. The last time we'd seen each other I'd slammed the door to that old house on my way out after she told me that my man wasn't trustworthy, that he'd already left one woman.

"I think you made the right choice with Robert. After so many fiascos I was worried you'd inherited my bad luck with men," she said.

I didn't know what to say, so I chuckled and picked up some papers from the doctor that were on her nightstand. It made me sad that after all this time she was only able to respect me after she'd hurt me and forced me to stand up for myself.

"Your father wasn't a bad person," she continued. "Years later, the only thing that pains me is that he didn't leave you anything in his will. When I saw that he'd left everything to his mother, I wanted to kill him." I was already starting to feel dizzy from hearing that story, always that same story, when she held out her hand to me. "But money isn't everything. The fact that after all we've been through you turned out so well… that truly makes me feel at peace."

I said goodbye soon after that, but not before writing down in great detail all the medicines she had to take and repeating that if anything happened, she should call me, that I'd be there in less than three hours. I would have come in the rain, barefoot, limping. And yet, being there made me feel upended. So much so that I didn't know if

I would make it to Barcelona. And while I was thinking about where I could make a stop on the way, maybe at the dwarf nun's convent or maybe at that inn I vaguely recalled from when I was a schoolgirl, I looked at her for the last time from the hallway: one arm in a sling, her neck rigid, and with that narrow field of vision she'd always had, in that same windowless room where she'd been born and where she'd likely die.

From the entryway I heard her calling out: "Say hi to Robert for me. Hope to see you both soon! Drive safely in the fog! And don't forget to write to that library!"

When I got into the car, I couldn't stop crying.